Three Murder Mysteries

Mystery Dinner Theatre Scripts

with a concluding chapter on producing and performing mystery dinner theatre shows

By John P. Palmer, London, Ontario, CANADA
©Copyright 2019

Three Murder Mysteries

This book contains the scripts for three mystery dinner theatre plays, designed to be performed during a meal with the actors interacting in character with members of the audience the entire time.

Two of the three scripts in the book are variations on the same basic script adapted to two different holiday seasons.

All three of the scripts have been written for a cast of five actors.

All of the scripts contain innuendo and are best-suited for mature audiences.

Please note that, as is typical for published play scripts, purchase of a script does not grant production rights for the play to the purchaser or anyone else who might have a copy of the script. There is a royalty fee of $25 [US] or $30 [Canadian] required for each performance of each play.

Royalty payments should be sent via Interac e-transfer to the playwright, John Palmer, at eclectecon@gmail.com , or email me at that address to make other arrangements or if you have any questions.

Brief Descriptions of the Plays

Murder at the Office Christmas Party

It's time for the annual Christmas party at Arttekko *[pronounced ar-TECH-oh]*, a firm that produces and distributes thousands of art prints to hotels, motels, and commercial buildings every year. Betty Batchly, the CEO, inherited the firm when her husband died over a decade ago, and she has been the driving force behind Arttekko's success. She is so compelled to be successful that she angers everyone around her, some of whom are either not nice at all or too nice to be believed. Who dies? Who kills the victim and how? Among this group of highly driven business people, they all have motives. Surely someone should be able to solve the case...

Murder at the Office New Year's Eve Party

The same basic script with appropriate changes made for the New Year's Eve. This version has one big advantage – many of the props for it can be bought on sale after Christmas.

Cast for both of the above scripts:
Betty Batchly. Bossy, aggressive. Age range 45-65
Tim Jones. Ambitious, slimy. Age range 35-55
Elizabeth Hurd. Competent, caring,. Age range 35-50
David Dekker. Meek, gofer, unambitious. Age range 40 -65
Geri Elliot. Manipulator, crooked. Age range 30-55

Shrink-Wrapped Murder

Following dinner, there is to be a panel discussion or symposium during which four panellists will present their research papers on new topics in the psychology of sexual relations. The audience is a group of residents, interns, students, media members, plus a bunch of others (i.e. the audience members) who seem slightly more than intrigued with sex talk in the guise of academic pursuits.

Dr. Sigmoid Frond (age range 50 - 85), an arrogant over-the-hill former leader in the field of the psychology of sex, will be chairing the symposium. Through the scenes and audience interactions with actors between the scenes, it becomes apparent that Dr. Frond has more than likely been:
- Extorting/blackmailing/somehow pressuring the others
- Possibly double billing for clients
- Padding expense accts
- Sleeping with patients
- Stealing patients from the other therapists
- Lying about the ethics of the other therapists
  …. And more!

The panel has been organized by Phillipa MaGraw (Age range 35 - 60), who is the loyal and energetic research and executive assistant of Dr. Sigmoid Frond. In addition to Dr. Frond, the others scheduled to appear on the panel are:

Dr. Ruthie Westover – brash, outspoken, flirty. Age range 25-40
Dr. Andrew Johnson – naïve, not quite with it. Age range 30-50
Dr. Robin Bobbitt – smarmy, glib, media savvy. Age 30-60

All have a motive for killing Dr. Frond.

Table of Contents

Brief descriptions of the plays 3
Murder at the Office Christmas Party 6
Shrink-Wrapped Murder 36
Murder at the Office New Year's Eve Party 64
Other Holiday Variations 92

An Introduction to Producing and Performing Mystery Dinner Theatre Shows 93
    Timing and Structure............................ 94
    Guide for Actors 96
    Guide for Directors 98
    Audience Participation 100
    General 101
    Solution Slips 102
Acknowledgements 103

Murder at the Office Christmas Party

It's time for the annual Christmas party at Arttekko *[ar-TECH-oh]*, a firm that produces and distributes thousands of art prints to hotels, motels, and commercial buildings every year. Betty Batchly, the CEO, inherited the firm when her husband died over a decade ago, and she has been the driving force behind Arttekko's success. She is so compelled to be successful that she angers everyone around her, some of whom are either not nice at all or too nice to be believed. Who dies? Who kills the victim and how? Among this group of highly driven business people, they all have motives. Surely someone should be able to solve the case…

Copyright, 2019, John P. Palmer ©
This play is adaptable for other holidays quite easily. A version for New Year's Eve is provided here as the third mystery dinner theatre play. Other variations are described at the end of this play for Valentine's Day, St. Patrick's Day, Easter, Victoria Day, Canada Day, Hallowe'en, or Thanksgiving.

Character Descriptions

Betty Batchly:
Betty is the CEO of Arttekko, a corporation that sells mass-produced artwork in batches of hundreds, even thousands, to hotels and corporations. She buys up the rights to photos or artwork to use for her business, but mostly she uses artwork that is no longer protected by copyright. At times, however, she has been known to use some artwork without properly acquiring the rights, and then she feigns ignorance if anyone complains.

Betty is a very driven entrepreneur. She built her business after her late husband's printing business went belly up. She says, "It went 'butt up', not 'belly up'. He fell flat on his face with his butt up in the air because he couldn't keep up with the times." Betty has a large production, warehouse, and shipping facility in a nearby small town [e.g. Thamesford] where they print the art, frame it, and ship it in lots no smaller than two dozen each. She has an extensive online catalogue to choose from, and her prices are very low because she standardized her prints to only four different sizes. But she is facing increasing threats of competition from foreign suppliers or from North American firms that produce the art abroad and ship it from there.

Betty is honest but tough. She is so driven that she seems cruel and hard. She is late 40s - early 60s, sharp mentally, and sharp-tongued. At one time or another, she has clearly antagonized everyone who has ever worked with or for her.

[Victim]

Tim Jones:

Tim is a business school product who thinks he knows more than he does and thinks he is more capable than he is. He keeps telling people that he knows the company could make more money if only they would [import more foreign-produced art; or use 3-D printers to print the artwork and the frames all in one piece; or spend more money on wining and dining hotel and office building executives; or hold more exhibitions for the hotel and resort business managers, etc.].

Tim is macho, slick, and ambitious. He fully anticipates he will be made Vice President of Arttekko within the next year or sooner. Failing that he's sure he will have no problem finding an executive position elsewhere. As the evening wears on, it becomes clear that Betty has no interest in promoting him. He is furious and makes vague threats that people would ordinarily believe are made only in the heat of the moment. Age range: early 30s to early 50s. Tim is married (to **AUD #3** from the audience).

[Motive: upset at not being promoted faster]

Elizabeth Hurd:

Elizabeth is a hard-working, mildly ambitious senior manager at Arttekko. She and Tim compete to show who is better, smarter, and kinder when kindness is called for. She's a bit of a geek. She resents and is even jealous of Tim's veneer of confidence, but she also knows she should have more authority and decision-making power in the firm than she does. She defers to Tim but makes very negative, snide remarks about him when he isn't around.

Elizabeth has had an ongoing secret relationship with the older David, the long-time stockboy/mailroom/gofer for the firm. They have matching rings that they wear on their right hands "Oh these? Just a coincidence I guess."

Elizabeth received her business training at the local for-profit college, Thames College. She knows the training wasn't very good, but she also has finally realized she has more smarts and ability than Tim. Age 30s – 50.

[Motive: she knows she deserves more recognition for her abilities, and she resents that both she and David are being put down all the time.]

David Dekker:
>David was hired by Betty's late husband and has been with the firm since long before Betty expanded it from being a printing shop into being a global art supplier. He is mild-mannered, meek, kind, and helpful. He looks after the mail, the coffee, the stockroom, etc. He is generally a suck-up gofer. Elizabeth is smarter and more ambitious than David, but she is drawn to his kind personality. He loves looking after Elizabeth and doesn't like the fact that Betty seems not to appreciate her. Also David doesn't like the fact that Tim seems to be outmaneuvering Elizabeth in the game of corporate politics. Betty and Tim think David is a wimp and treat him that way. Age range 40s to late 50s.

[Motive: resents Betty's treatment of both Elizabeth and himself]

Geraldine [or Geri] Elliot:
>Geri is the somewhat shady major purchasing agent for the global letoM Motel chain. She spends hundreds of thousands of dollars on art for her chain each year, and in that capacity, she controls the purchasing decisions of the largest customer for Arttekko. Betty knows that Geri pads her expenses and takes kickbacks from the suppliers; Betty has evidence of this. Geri's job will be in jeopardy if Betty blows the whistle on her. So long as letoM Motels keep buying art from Arttekko, Betty won't do that, but the stress and worry are getting Geri down. Age range open.

[Motive: afraid that Betty will tell letoM about bribes and expense-account padding]

Costumes

Generally, the costumes should be Christmas party type garb. Christmas neckties with white shirts for the men and Christmassy clothing in general.

Guests should be encouraged to dress in festive costumes themselves: Christmas sweaters, elf ears, elf hats, Santa hats, Christmas earrings, mistletoe headbands, etc.

In the first three scenes, David is wearing a sport coat that presumably is covering the gun he has in the back of his waistband (although it might be good to wait until Scene 4 for him to put it there).

Murder at the Office Christmas Party

Scene 1

*[There must be a table or suitable space to put the Christmas tree and cake. David will bring in the tree during **this** scene but will bring in the cake and knife later.*

*Before the show begins, **David** selects a table and designates four of the people at that table to be the singers known as "The Artichokes", rehearses them briefly, and shows them the dance moves for Winter Wonderland.*

*[Also prior to the scene, **Tim**, and **Geri**, should select appropriate audience members to be their spouses.]*

Prior to the scene, David should interact with the audience, but he should leave the room before the scene begins.]

Betty: Good evening, everyone, and welcome to our annual Christmas party for Arttekko. We're so glad you could all be here to celebrate our continued success. We know **we** wouldn't be here if it weren't for all of **you!**

Later this evening, as we are concluding dinner, we will have our traditional tree-lighting ceremony. At that time, we will dim the room lights and **then**, just as we turn on the tree lights, we will all pop our Christmas poppers or blow on your noisemakers. Even though it's tempting to pull your popper right now or blow one of those things, please wait until we turn out the room lights and give you the go ahead.

David: *[Entering with small tree; garland and lights already on it.]* Excuse me, Ms. Batchly, here's the Christmas tree. Should I put it here on the table?

Betty: *[tersely]* That'll be fine, David. Did you test the lights to make sure they work?

David: Yes, I did, Ms. Batchly. Here, I'll show you *[moves to turn on the lights]*.

Betty: *[Shouts]* **NO!!!** Don't turn them on yet, not in here. You know I don't want them turned on until the proper time!

David: *[meekly]* Yes, Ma'am.

Elizabeth: David, I've saved a place for you to sit over here with me.

David: Thanks, Elizabeth, I'd like that, but I already have a place over there with the Artichokes *[the company choir]*.

Elizabeth: Okay. Well, when you're finished there with the tree could you please bring me a drink?

David: Sure. *[Bustles around the tree a bit, then gets drinks for Elizabeth and Tim (see below)].*

Tim: *[sarcastically]* He's such a good helper. More like a mascot for Arttekko than an employee. And just about as productive. Hey, David, bring me a drink, too, will ya?

Eliz.: Stop that, Tim! David does lots of things for everyone here at Arttekko.

Betty: *[sternly].* You two! This is supposed to be a party, not a snipe session. *[To audience]*... And one of the reasons we can keep partying and being successful as a firm involves our close working relationship with the worldwide chain of letoM *[pronounced 'Let 'em']* Motels. LetoM Motels knows they can count on Arttekko to deliver appropriate artwork for all their interiors, on time, and error-free. And here from letoM Motels to help us celebrate Christmas this year is our primary letoM contact Geri Eliot. *[Leads applause]*

Geri: Thanks, Betty. And thanks for inviting me. The relationship between LetoM and Arttekko is a two-way street. We all benefit from it in many ways.

Betty: Thanks, Geri.
[to room] As you all know, my late husband Norman Batchly started our firm nearly forty years ago when he bought Kelly Printing. Without Norman's early efforts we all wouldn't be here today, celebrating at our annual Christmas party. So please join me in a toast, to Norman. *[Raises glass]*

Others: *[loudly]* To Norman.

David: *[sneezes into clean handkerchief and blows nose.]*

Eliz.: Bless you.

David: Thanks, Elizabeth.

Betty: *[interrupting]* And now let's also keep in mind that it was only because of our expansion into the mass-produced art business that we have all thrived as Kelly Printing evolved and grew into Arttekko. To Arttekko.

Others: *[loudly]* To Arttekko.

Scene 2

[Audience Card #1]
    Go up to Geri Eliot of letoM Motels and ask, "Geri Eliot, How did LetoM get its name?"

Geri: Perhaps you've already figured out that "LetoM" *[says the letters separately]* …L…E…T…O…M is just "motel" spelled backwards. The founder of the chain thought of the name so that when he put up neon lights on top of the motels, the signs would say "letoM Motel" from either direction.

But when people started making jokes about, "What does 'motel' say backwards?" we captured an entire market of people who thought a motel named "Let 'em" would rent rooms by the hour.

*[To **AUD #1**]* Have you ever stayed at one of our motels? *[Wait for answer; and whatever they answer, continue "and why not?" or "what did you think of it?"]*

Tim: Hey Geri, it's good to see you again. Too bad things didn't work out for us to spend more time together or maybe even 'go bowling' at the trade show in Las Vegas last year, but here you are now…

Geri: *[interrupting]* I was at the trade show on business, Tim, and I'm here on business, too. So just cool it, will you?

Betty: *[Glares at Tim; then speaks to Geri]* And we're glad to have you here, too, Geri. Thanks again for coming.

But I did want to ask you about something, Geri. I've been sending you "finders' fees" for the past six years to thank you for finding us and directing all of LetoM's business our way. But I got a notice last month from LetoM's head office that they do not charge finders' fees and that we are not to pay any person or agent a finders' fee.

Geri: Yeah, well….

Betty: So does this mean you've been cheating your bosses by extorting a payoff from us and from your other suppliers?

Geri: It's not extortion. It is a finders' fee --- a fee you've been very happy to pay and that you'll keep paying if you want to keep our business.

Betty: *[threateningly].* Maybe we should talk about this some more, Geri. Maybe letoM doesn't want to keep employees around who are extracting bribes from their suppliers. Maybe letoM would deeply appreciate my letting them know about your shady practices. Maybe they would show their gratitude by giving Arttekko a long-term contract. And maybe as a result, you would be blackballed in the industry. And so maybe we need to renegotiate your finder's fee, Geri.

Geri: Maybe. But then again maybe not. Let's not forget that you were eager to pay these finder's fees to get our business; you are every bit as culpable as we are. And then there was all the flirting you did with my husband *[a pre-selected audience member]* two years ago, right **[call Audience #2 by name]**? *[Give Aud #2 card to read].*

Audience Card #2
Let's not be hasty, Geri. She was just checking to see if I had any loose change in my pockets. ... And later, that position we were in? Remember we were playing Twister. It wasn't what it looked like.

Geri: Right.... And I'm supposed to believe that? Especially about a woman who bribes purchasing agents and who would do anything to grow her business? Well just don't be letting her grow ***your*** business if you know what's good for you.

David: *[sneezes into handkerchief again, blows nose again; exits]*

Scene 3

David: *[entering from outside the room, wiping nose]* Excuse me, Ms. Batchly, but you've received a fax.

Betty: *[impatiently]* Give it to Elizabeth. You know she looks after all our communications.

David: Yes, Ma'am. …. *[to Elizabeth]* Here, Elizabeth. *[David gazes overly-obviously and lovingly into her eyes as he hands her the fax.]*

Eliz.: Thank you, David. *[Holds some mistletoe over his head and kisses him on his cheek]* You do so much around here.

David: Thanks, Elizabeth. *[Touches her arm lovingly and shuffles off].*

Eliz.: Oh!! Ms. Batchly this looks important. I think you should read it now.

Betty: Read it out aloud. We have no secrets.

Eliz.: Okaayyyy *[reluctant]*. It's from the purchasing agent of Redner Hotels. He says they have a quote from a foreign firm to do the artwork for 30% less than we are charging.

Betty: That's nothing new. We'll deal with it in the morning. The main thing is that all our customers get exactly what they want from us in a matter of days, and they know the quality of our product. They also know we will deal with any problems immediately. And *[glaring at various members of the audience]* everyone working for Arttekko knows that heads will roll if things go wrong.

Geri: 30% lower prices? I'll have to call Redner to see what that's about?

Betty: You do that…and see what happens to your career in this business.

None of this foreign competition will have much effect on us…yet… Those companies take three months to deliver their artwork, and if there are problems…. Well, it takes another six months to resolve anything with those firms. We're much better situated to provide speedy and high-quality service. *[To Geri]* And you know it!

Tim: But Betty, the foreign production costs are so low. I wonder if maybe we should consider shifting some of our own larger-scale production there…

Betty: Tim, I know you have a business degree, but that doesn't mean you know enough to make these decisions. Not yet. *[Sighs.]* Next week we can take **another** look at all the costs involved if you insist, but I'm sure you're wrong.

Tim: But using foreign producers is the wave of the future, Betty. I'm sure that after I'm promoted to Vice President, as we discussed when I was hired, we will want to re-open this issue.

Betty: *[cautiously]* Yes, Tim, when we hired you, we did talk about the upside potential for you here at Arttekko. I think it's probably still there, but just not yet.

Tim: Not yet!!??? What does that mean? If not now, when?

Betty: You need to mature into the job, Tim. But here at the Christmas party isn't the time or place to discuss this.

Tim: Okay, but don't expect a person with my abilities to wait too long…. *[A veiled threat]*

David *[David collects The Artichokes and Tim at the end of Scene 3 and takes them out to prepare costumes and to rehearse.]*

Scene 4

*[Before entering, **David** places gun in back of his waistband.]*

Betty: And now, for our evening's entertainment, here is the Arttekko company choir --- "The Artichokes"!

David *[leads Artichokes in, all carrying top hats behind their backs and wearing Christmas scarves and dark glasses. All are carrying and gently ringing very small and quiet-ish sleigh bells.]*

David and Tim are in the middle, David is conducting and leading the dance steps as The Artichokes sing and dance:

Sleigh bells ring, *[left foot out and back]* are you listening *[left foot out and back]*
In the lane, *[right foot out and back]* snow is glistening *[right foot out and back]*
A beautiful sight *[empty hand up above eyes, as if peering]*
We're happy tonight *[big smiles]*
Walking in a winter wonderland *[walking in place]*

Gone away *[left foot out and back]* is the bluebird *[left foot out and back]*
Here to stay *[right foot out and back]* is a new bird *[right foot out and back]*
He sings a love song *[empty hand over heart]*
As we go along
Walking in a winter wonderland *[walking in place]*

*[The Artichokes put on hats, then **Tim** puts a carrot in **David**'s mouth]*

In the meadow we can build a snowman
And pretend that he is Parson Brown
He'll say, Are you married?
We'll say, No man

David: *[Removes carrot from his mouth and stops The Artichokes (and stops the audience if they are singing along). When they are quiet, David continues (speaking or singing the line here)]* That last line we sang was "He'll say, 'Are you married? We'll say, No man.'"

Take it, Tim!

Tim: *[sings or speaks, depending on actor's comfort zone]*
Cuz all we want to do is fool around…

David: Everyone now *[same dance steps]*:

> Later on, we'll perspire
> As we dream by the fire
> To face unafraid *[hands cup each side of face]*
> The plans that we've made
> Walking in a winter wonderland

Eliz.: *[leads the applause but then stops abruptly, shouting as David starts to lead the choir out of the room].* **David!! I can see that gun! Did you have to bring it here? Tonight?**

David: *[pulls gun from the back of his waistband, where people probably were able to see it when he was conducting].* I carry it everywhere, Elizabeth; you know that. I always want to be prepared in case a mass shooter tries to take out a large group of people.

Eliz: I know, David, and I'm glad you're around, ready to protect us all, but this is Christmas, David.

David: What better time for a mass shooter to attack? I think everyone here can relax just a bit knowing that I'm here with a gun.

Eliz: Well, maybe... *[David exits with The Artichokes to put props away. Tim and David "forget" to leave scarves with the rest of the props and are wearing them for the next few scenes.]*

Scene 5

[After The Artichokes return to the room]

Betty: Thank you again Artichokes. *[Leads applause **un**excitedly]* Good work, David. It's good to see you can do **something** right around here.

Eliz: What do you mean, Ms. Batchly? David does a lot of things right around here. So do all of us!

Betty: Maybe, but there are also several things that don't get done right around here, too. If Arttekko is going to survive the onslaught from foreign competition, we're all going to have to work harder and more carefully. Right? *[Glaring at audience]* Or do you all want your jobs out-sourced to foreign producers right now?

Others: *[grumbling randomly]* Right, yes Ms. Batchly, uh huh, if you say so.

Betty: And while we're on the topic of getting things right, Elizabeth, the sales projection figures you produced for us last month were off by ten percent. Our profit margins are very thin, and we need to schedule production carefully so that we don't end up paying all these yahoos *[gestures to the audience]* for just standing around. Your errors led to some serious cost increases for Arttekko, Elizabeth. You'll have to do better.

Eliz: I know, Ms. Batchly. But the sales projection figures for the entire North American industry were off by even more than 10% last month. My predictions were better than most…

Tim: Remember what Yogi Berra said, "It's really hard to predict, especially about the future."

Betty: Be quiet, Tim. We can do without your little attempts at humour. Missing sales forecasts is a serious problem. You would know that if you paid more attention to your own work at Arttekko.

Elizabeth, this past month, you estimated the sales would be lower than they were, and to make sure we got the artwork produced and shipped out on time, Arttekko had to hire a bunch of these bozos here to work overtime and on weekends. That was **very** costly!

Eliz: I know, Ms. Batchly, I'm doing everything I can to narrow the margins for error.

Geri: What's the problem, Elizabeth? You know our orders from letoM Motels well in advance. Aren't all the contracts negotiated well ahead of production time?

Eliz: Of course they are! But last month we had a huge rush order from Trump Hotels. Given their reputation for not paying bills, we delayed work on the order until we had an 80% deposit. It took a lot of time to squeeze the deposit out of those misers, and by the time we got the deposit, we had to rush the production to meet the deadline for delivery.

Tim: *[almost creepily]* I think you've done pretty well with the forecasts, Elizabeth, but let me know if you ever want to stay late to work on them a bit more together.

Betty: Tim! If you're interested in staying late to work on things here at Arttekko, you should consider working harder and longer on your own assignments.

Audience #3 (Tim's wife) stands and shrieks:
What? You mean Tim **hasn't** been working late every night this past month as he said? Tim, you scoundrel! You've been out bowling again, haven't you! You dirty donkey! You promised you wouldn't do that anymore ......*[pause, smile flirtatiously]*.... not without taking me along. *[She and Tim laugh together].*

[David exits sometime before next scene]

Scene 6

David *[brings in frosted Christmas cake, along with a knife, rum, and cigarette lighter;* **approaches** *Betty]*
Excuse me Ms. Batchly. Here's the Christmas cake that we always have after we light the Christmas tree. I have the knife here for cutting it, plenty of rum, and a cigarette lighter so we can light up the rum to flambé all the pieces as they're cut. Where should I put all these things?

Betty: *[Impatiently].* It doesn't matter. Put them somewhere handy.

David: Yes, Ma'am. I'll put them on the table next to the tree, okay?

Betty: *[Sticks her finger in the frosting and then licks her finger.]* Eww. That frosting tastes even worse this year than it did last year. Find a better supplier next year, David.

Eliz: Ms. Batchly, do you think that maybe in the spirit of Christmas, you could show a bit more love and kindness tonight?

Betty: Love, schmove. That's no way to run a business.

Tim: Speaking of love, Elizabeth….

Eliz: Forget it, Tim! Don't be such a creep. And don't even think of coming near me with any mistletoe.

Tim: Relax, Elizabeth. When I said "speaking of love", I meant that I've noticed you and David have matching rings and that you two stand up for each other all the time. What's that all about?

Eliz: David is a nice man, and he doesn't get the credit he deserves for everything he does here.

David: Neither do you, Elizabeth. I think that deep down Betty knows you're an excellent business manager and market analyst.

Eliz: Well… She doesn't seem to value any of us at all.

Tim: You're right about that, Elizabeth, Betty doesn't really value any of us; and that had better change soon!

But that doesn't explain those matching rings. What's the story there? Huh? *[Leers a bit?]*

Eliz: Oh, these? David bought one when he was in Hamilton on holidays last year. I admired it, so I ordered one like it. It's just a coincidence, Tim. We both happen to like the same rings.

Tim: Yeah sure.

Scene 7 *[after dinner but before dessert]*

Betty: Well, everybody, the time has come to light the tree! When the room lights go down, everyone who has a popper can go ahead and pull it; and those of you with noise makers can blow them. But please wait until the room lights go down before pulling your poppers or blowing your things! And maybe in the sharing spirit of Christmas, those of you who have poppers can get a friend or partner who doesn't have one to pull your popper with you…

Elizabeth, Tim, and David, you three usually help with the lighting ceremony. And Geri, why don't you join us, too?

[Elizabeth, Tim, David, and Geri all gather around the tree]

Betty: And now can we have the room lights off, please! *[After lights go down]* Okay, folks, let's pull those poppers and blow those noise makers!!

Sound cue: play "o Christmas Tree" reasonably loudly!

There is total confusion in the dark, as...

- The sound of Christmas poppers going off and noise makers being used.
- *Betty* applies blood to her neck and is lying on the floor (or sitting in a chair, but propped such that the wound is easy to examine).]
- *Elizabeth* removes tinsel garland from tree.
- *Tim* gently tips the tree over.
- *Elizabeth* dumps the tinsel garland in a pile onto the tree.
- *Geri* sets the knife on the floor.
- *David* shoots gun toward tree and places gun on the floor.
- Cast members all shouting and mumbling.
- *Tim* is holding his scarf, not wearing it.

David: *[Checks to make sure everyone else is ready then shouts].* Something doesn't seem right here! Can we please have the lights back on?

Geri: *[Waits for lights to come on. Looks at Betty and shouts almost disgustedly]* Oh No! *[Pause]* Oh, for crying out loud, this is just what I don't need. It looks as if Betty has been shot in the dark. I don't have time for this nonsense.

Tim: Shot! David, you have a gun! Why did you shoot Betty?

David: I didn't! When the lights went off, I felt a shove on my back. I put my hand back there, and my gun was gone! Someone took it from my waistband. I didn't shoot it, and I didn't shoot Betty.

Tim: Yeah, you're probably too much of a wimp to actually kill someone anyway.

Eliz: But you aren't, are you, Tim! You knew that gun was there in David's waistband, and you easily could have pushed David, taken his gun, and shot Betty while everyone was pulling their poppers and making noise.

Geri: Are we sure she was shot? I mean look – the Christmas tree is tipped over. The tinsel garland was clearly removed and then just tossed back onto the tree. Maybe she was strangled with that garland. Or look! Tim isn't wearing his scarf any more, the one he had on when he was singing. He has it in his hand! Maybe he strangled her with that! Nice work, Tim!

Tim: Well, David still has his scarf with him, too. Maybe he strangled her instead of shooting her.

Eliz: And the knife has been moved; *[looks and sees it]* it's on the floor now! Maybe she was stabbed! And look! David's gun is there on the floor, too!

David: I think she was shot, **and not by me!** Strangling wouldn't have caused that wound on her neck. And if she'd been stabbed, why isn't there any blood on the knife?

Geri: Maybe the tinsel or Tim's scarf chafed her neck and caused that wound. *[pause]* Or, maybe she was poisoned?

Eliz: Poisoned? How and when?

Geri: The frosting on the cake! She dipped her finger into that, remember, and said it tasted worse than usual! Anyone could have poisoned it before David brought it in.

Tim: That would have poisoned any one of us, not just her. *[Gasp]* or maybe **all** of us! I'm not touching that cake now. Don't eat the cake, people!

Eliz: *[pondering]* David, I think you're right. She was probably shot, but how do we know which one of us shot her? Tim, you were angry because she was delaying your promotion. Did you shoot her?

Tim: Hey, I didn't like her, but she paid me well. Also, I respected her business skills and admired her toughness. Yes, I was upset that she wasn't promoting me fast enough, but I was already exploring other career options. I didn't need her. Besides, if I killed her, who's to say I'd be promoted after that? Huh? So, no, I didn't kill her.... But Geri, she threatened you pretty seriously tonight. Maybe you killed her.

Geri: I wasn't bothered by her threats. We were just negotiating, that's all. But what about this nicey-nice lady *[indicating Elizabeth]*? Betty was seriously on her case tonight for not getting the sales forecasts right, and she was feeling as if Betty didn't give her proper recognition for all she did in the firm.

Tim: Speaking of proper recognition, David was always defending Elizabeth, and she was always talking about how much **he** was under-appreciated. Maybe Mr. Wimp here grew a pair and did it himself, but pretended someone else took the gun from his waistband.

David: *[Sneezes, but into his elbow, not his handkerchief!]* Everyone here had good reason to be happy that Betty is dead. But instead of speculating wildly, let's see if we can solve this murder. We'll put all the evidence we can find up here on this table. Then each of you come up and look at the body **without touching it!** And look at the evidence. Then fill out your suggestion slips: Who killed Betty the Batchly and how?

Evidence list:
- *Gun from floor [don't let people pick this up]*
- *Knife from floor*
- *Christmas tree tipped over*
- *Tinsel dumped onto tree*
- *Tim's scarf*
- *David's scarf*
- *Christmas cake*
- *Also on the table: rum and cigarette lighter [Hint: make sure the rum is heavily guarded!]*

Denouement
[David makes sure he has bloody handkerchief in his pocket]

Eliz: Okay, everyone. Let's face it. We all liked having a job and we all liked the paycheques from Arttekko, but none of us liked Betty. Every one of her employees here in this room had a good strong motive for killing her. Even __**AUD #4**__ here could have killed her. S/he was bad-mouthing Betty all night. Where were you, **AUD #4**, when the lights went out? *[Check with AUD#4's seat neighbours for verification; maybe even grill **AUD #4** a bit].*

Geri: So are you folks saying we'll have to stay here and give witness statements for the cops? I'm not sticking around for all this silliness. I'm a busy woman, and I have more important things to do. *[begins to slowly collect her belongings but doesn't leave.].*

David: *[sneezes again, and without thinking, pulls bloody handkerchief out to blow his nose].*

Eliz: Bless you.

David: Thank you, Elizabeth.

Geri: What is this? Some kind of love fest, you two?

Tim: Hey, everyone! Look at David's handkerchief! It has blood all over it!

Geri: Tim is right! David, how did your handkerchief get all bloody? It was perfectly clean when you blew your nose earlier this evening.

Tim: Well, not clean, Geri. He **did** blow his nose in it.

Eliz: David is very susceptible to getting bloody noses, right David? *[pause]* David??

David: Thanks for trying, Elizabeth. But no, I'm not susceptible to getting nosebleeds. I think it's time to fess up.

Eliz: *[rushing to David]* No, David! Don't!

David: *[Brushing off Elizabeth.]*. It's no use Elizabeth. The rest of you might as well know: Elizabeth and I have had a close relationship now for over seven years. We were married, secretly, three years ago. Betty the Batch would **not** tolerate having employees married to each other, but neither of us wanted to quit our jobs, so we just kept our marriage secret.

Tim: What a couple of idiots! Everybody at Arttekko knew you two had something going. Why didn't you just live together and not get married?

David: Don't call us idiots. We seriously considered that, but we knew that living common law would mean we'd have been married legally after only three years. Betty the Batch wouldn't have tolerated that either.

Eliz: David kept a small apartment that he used once in awhile, and we've been car-pooling to work together ever since I joined Arttekko, so no one suspected we were leaving from my apartment every morning to come to work.

Tim: We **all** *[gestures to audience]* **knew** there was something going on between you two. You didn't hide it very well. Betty knew, too. She even asked me about it just last week.

Eliz: And I'm sure you were happy to fan the flames of suspicion, weren't you, Tim. Anything to get ahead in the firm.

Geri: Whoa! Enough! I need to get out of here, so can we go back to the murder? Tell us about the blood on your handkerchief, David.

David: I was becoming increasingly upset with Betty the Batch. And tonight when she so rudely ordered me around in front of everyone and then criticized Elizabeth in front of everyone, too, I resolved to kill her. When the lights went out, I was ready to reach for my gun, but just then, someone shoved me. They must have taken my gun then.

Geri: That was me. I knew she would report that I was accepting pay-offs and padding my expense account for letoM Motels, and I couldn't let her do that. So I pushed you and took the gun. I hesitated a moment or so, and then I was bumped just as I fired the gun. I thought I'd shot her anyway, but, David if you have blood on your handkerchief, maybe something else happened.

Tim: I think you missed her, Geri. While you were getting the gun from David, I was trying to take the tinsel garland from the tree so I could strangle her. That Batch…ly wasn't going to promote me and I wanted revenge. But just as I got the garland off the tree, the gun went off and the tree fell down. I panicked and threw the garland back onto the tree. I never had a chance to strangle the Batch…ly.

Eliz: So that's when you took your scarf off! You still were going to try to strangle her! And Geri's shot from David's gun must have hit the tree, knocking it over. I knew you didn't shoot her, David!

David: You're right, Elizabeth! There's a bullet lodged into the tree right here *[indicating bullet in tree upright pole]*.

Geri: Exactly what did you do after I took your gun, David?

David: I could tell Betty hadn't been hit by the gunshot because she was still babbling about something as the tree fell.

[turns to Elizabeth] Darling, I couldn't take it anymore. She was never very pleasant to me in spite of everything I did for the company. And she didn't treat you any better. Yesterday she confronted me about our relationship. I denied everything, of course, to save our jobs, but she seemed even more menacing than usual. After she publicly criticized your work tonight, I snapped. I'm sorry.

Tim: Hey, the wimp has a pair after all! Way to go, David! What happened? How'd you do it?

David: You're the smart guy with the biz-skool degree. You haven't figured it out yet?

[pause]

Eliz: When you realized Geri's shot missed her, that's when you picked up the knife and stabbed her, right? *[David nods]* And then you wiped the knife clean with your handkerchief, right? *[David nods]* and when you tried to put the knife back on the table, it fell onto the floor. *[David nods again]* And the first time you sneezed after stabbing her, you remembered to sneeze into your elbow, not your handkerchief, but this second time you forgot and pulled out the bloody handkerchief.

David: I always knew you were the real brains here at Arttekko, Elizabeth, but now I'll have to leave. Will you go to the police station with me? I think they'll go easy on me when we call this entire roomful of witnesses to testify that Geri and Tim and **AUD#4** were all trying to kill her, too.

Eliz: I'll go with you, David, but not to the police station. Over the years, I've been putting away our retirement savings. We can transfer those to a bank in the Caribbean and find an island to live on there where we can retire together. Let's get out of here before the police are called. *Elizabeth takes David's arm and leads him out the door.}*

Tim: *[lewd leer]* Say, Geri you know any places around here to go … bowling?

Geri: Zip it up, Tim. You'd have to kill me first. *[exits]*.

Tim: *[shouting after Geri]:* Hey, I'm not into necrophilia, Geri, but if you are, there's a body here in the room…. *[exits]*

*** The End ***

Solution:

David did it with the knife. He had two motives: (1) he couldn't take her badgering him and Elizabeth; (2) also, he became concerned when Betty confronted him about his relationship with Elizabeth. Before the denouement, the audience will likely be aware of only the first one because the second one is revealed only in the denouement.

Props

General:
- Dozens (? Some? Urge customers to bring/provide their own?) of Christmas poppers/crackers.
- Tiny party horns.
- Crappy mass-produced art to show Arttekko's products

David's responsibility *[he'll need help before the show, obviously]*:
- Small(ish?) battery powered Christmas tree with lights, and with bullet lodged in the upright portion of the tree. Lights don't have to work, actually, since they're never turned on during the show.
- Tinsel garland on tree.
- Fax from Redner Hotels
- 6 sets of Jingle bells, scarves, dark glasses, and top hats for song.
- Carrot for song
- Gun
- Frosted Christmas cake
- Knife for cutting Christmas cake
- Handkerchief with blood smeared on it for David
- Clean handkerchief for David
- Rum
- Cigarette lighter

Tim: Mistletoe for Tim, possibly headband & mistletoe on springs?

Betty: Thick blood for neck.

Geri: Business cards

Elizabeth: mistletoe

Elizabeth and David: Matching rings

Audience Participation and Role Cards

AUDs #1 and #4 are chosen during the show.
AUDs #2 and #3 are chosen during the pre-show mingling
Also members of The Artichokes are chosen during pre-show mingling

Audience Card #1

Go up to Geri Eliot of letoM Motels and ask, "Excuse me, Geri. How did LetoM get its name?"
Do this <u>now</u> and BE VERY LOUD

Role Card for AUD #2

Your role: You are Geraldine Eliot's husband. She is a purchasing agent for letoM Motels, a major hotel chain. She has dragged you here because Arttekko is her best business connection, and it will look good for you to be with her. You know that Geraldine has been taking bribes from suppliers and padding her expense account. You know it's wrong, but the money is good. At the end, Geri will leave. It happens often that she leaves parties early, expecting you to find your own way home.

During the show also give **AUD #2** this card:

[**Stand up and be loud**] Well, let's not be hasty, Geri. Betty was just checking to see if I had any loose change in my pockets. And later, that position we were in?... remember we were playing Twister. It wasn't what it looked like.
Do this <u>now</u>

Role Card for AUD #3

Your role: You are Tim Jones's wife. He's a philanderer, but you don't mind. You two have an "open" marriage and like to swing in threesomes or with other couples. At one point in the evening, Tim will hand you a card to read. When he does, stand up and shriek very loudly as you read it.

Audience Card for AUD #3 *[handed out where indicated in script]*

What? You mean Tim **hasn't** been working late every night this past month the way he said? Tim, you scoundrel! You've been out bowling again, haven't you! You dirty donkey! You promised you wouldn't do that anymore ......*[pause, smile flirtatiously]*.... not without taking me along. *[She and Tim laugh together and sit down].*

Audience #4 is selected at the time called for in the script. There is no Audience card for AUD #4.

Possible attachment for fronts of the top hats:

Winter Wonderland Lyrics and Dance Steps

Sleigh bells ring *[left foot out and back]* are you listening *[left foot out and back]*
In the lane, *[right foot out and back]* snow is glistening *[right foot out and back]*
A beautiful sight *[empty hand up above eyes, as if peering]*
We're happy tonight
Walking in a winter wonderland *[walking in place]*

Gone away *[left foot out and back]* is the bluebird *[left foot out and back]*
Here to stay *[right foot out and back]* is a new bird *[right foot out and back]*
He sings a love song *[empty hand over heart]*
As we go along
Walking in a winter wonderland *[walking in place]*

> *[The Artichokes put on hats, then Tim puts a carrot in David's mouth]*

> In the meadow we can build a snowman
> And pretend that he is Parson Brown
> He'll say, Are you married?
> We'll say, No man

David *[Stops The Artichokes (and stops the audience if they are singing along). When they are quiet, David removes the carrot from his mouth and continues (speaking or singing the line here)]* That last line we sang was "He'll say, 'Are you married? We'll say, No man.'"

> Okay, Tim, you're on!

Tim: *[sings solo]*

David: Everyone now *[same dance steps]*:

> Later on, we'll perspire
> As we dream by the fire
> To face unafraid *[hands cup each side of face]*
> The plans that we've made
> Walking in a winter wonderland

Other holiday variations:

- **New Year's Eve:** This variation require very little change except to substitute a poster for the Christmas Tree. The script for New Year's Eve is part of this volume.

- **Valentine's Day**: A giant heart with red lights and garlands around the outside edge; possible song "Let me call you sweetheart"; hearts on top hats, heart-shaped eyeglasses, red scarves.

- **St. Patrick's Day**: A giant shamrock with green lights and garland around the outside edge; possible songs: march in to "It's a long way to Tipperary" and then sing "When Irish Eyes are Smiling". Shamrocks on hats or green hats; green lens glasses; green scarves.

- **Victoria Day**: A giant empty 2-4 with white lights around it and a silver garland; possible song "Canada" or "Roll out the Barrel". Canadian flags on top hats or red & white hats, or maybe even pictures of Queen Elizabeth on the hats; red lens glasses; red or red & white scarves.

- **Hallowe'en:** A giant pumpkin with orange streamers, garlands, and lights around it; possible song "The Monster Mash" or "Witch Doctor" or?. Jack-o-lanterns on top hats.

Shrink-Wrapped Murder

Setting: Following dinner, there is to be a panel discussion/symposium during which four panellists will present their research papers on new topics in psychology. The panel has been organized by Phillipa MaGraw, who is the loyal and energetic research and executive assistant of Dr. Sigmoid Frond, an over-the-hill former leader in the field. In addition to Dr. Frond, the others scheduled to appear on the panel are Dr. Ruthie Westover, Dr. Andrew Johnson, and Dr. Robin Bobbitt.

The Audience is a group of residents/interns/students/media, plus a bunch of people off the street (audience members) who are quite intrigued by sex talk in the guise of academic pursuits.

Through the scenes and audience interactions with actors between the scenes, it becomes apparent that Dr. Frond has more than likely been:

> Extorting/blackmailing/somehow pressuring the others
> Possibly double billing for clients
> Padding expense accts
> Sleeping with patients
> Stealing patients from the others
> Lying about the ethics of the other therapists
> …. And more!

All have a motive to kill him.

© **John P. Palmer, London, Ontario, 2018**

Cast of Characters

Dr. Sigmoid Frond is an arrogant older dean of the psychology profession. He did some Freudian research about 100 years ago (or so it seems), but it wasn't terribly important and he hasn't kept up-to-date in his field. However, he acts as if he still knows everything, and has done everything there is to be done in his field. He constantly gives condescending advice to everyone, referring to his "seminal piece" on the topic, whatever the topic might be. In addition to his research activities, which are in reality quite minimal even though he talks about them as if they are monumental and path-breaking, he has an active therapy practice. Most of his current published work involves little more than anecdotes about the clients he has seen, and he isn't too careful about their confidentiality. He wears a suit, sport coat, or blazer, along with dress pants, a dress shirt, and a necktie.

Phillipa MaGraw has worked for Frond for many years as a loyal administrator and research assistant. In fact, what little work Frond has published in the past twenty years was, in fact, based on research and notes written up by Phillipa. She organizes his appointments, writes up his notes, and organizes much of his daily life as well. She is loyal because he pays her well but mostly because she's afraid he'll reveal her own personal secrets to the others, there at the symposium and elsewhere. Underneath it all, she hates him, but she lets her feelings show only a little. She is quite attracted to Andy Johnson and tries to ingratiate herself with him. So she rushes around frenetically helping Frond (out of duty and fear) and Andy (out of attraction). Frond abuses her loyalty; Andy doesn't notice her special attentions because he's so interested in Ruthie. Phillipa carries a clipboard with a raft of notes and messages and a pen. She wears glasses that she keeps taking off and putting on. Business-style costume.

Dr. Ruthie Westover is an up-and-coming young turk in the psychology profession. The results of her research conflict markedly with those of Frond, and so everyone is eagerly awaiting the fireworks that are sure to explode during the panel discussion, if not before then. There have been allegations that she did some of her research by having sex with her patients/subjects. She is brash and outspoken. She sees Frond as an obstacle to step on as she climbs the professional ladder, sometimes flirting with him, other times cutting him to ribbons with her incisive sarcasm. She barely notices Phillipa, and she's considering whether and how to use Andy in some way. She is constantly provocative in every imaginable way.

Dr. Andy Johnson is a visiting psychologist from the Lichtenstein Institute for Psycho-Synthesis (LIPS) where he is on study leave from his home institution in Vancouver. He had wanted to devote his career to studying sexual behaviours in Rwanda, but his research was interrupted constantly by the civil strife in that country, so he has never quite been able to get started on, much less complete his *magnum opus*. Instead he drifted toward studying the social psychology of the Buhu [pronounced Boo Hoo] gangs in Vancouver and in Southeast Asia. In fact, he's not much of a researcher at all. He is at the symposium because of funding promised by Frond, and feels some obligation to be nice to Frond; he is also smitten with Ruthie and agrees with everything she says, no matter how inane she makes it, just to lead him along. He is very heavily into "feeling" and "getting in touch with one's inner self".

Dr. Robin Bobbitt [Probably male, but maybe could be female? (unlikely?)] hosts the afternoon television show "Round Pegs, Round Holes" providing advice, mostly to emotionally dysfunctional callers and live guests. He now calls himself a doctor, but received a PhD from The University of the Internet, which gave course credit for all of his talk show work. He is glib, but has very little formal training, so makes things up on the fly. The only reason people watch the show and call in for advice is because he is devilishly good-looking, has interesting guests on the show, and has a smooth manner with members of the opposite sex. Several years ago, he had "a relationship" with Ruthie, which she would like to forget, but of which Robin continues to remind her, in not-so-subtle ways.

Props List

Phillipa MaGraw
- Clipboard with note to Frond written in advance at bottom of papers
- Pen
- Nametags (if used) for Audience members plus Sharpie for writing names.
- [Scenes 1 and 2] five heavy coffee mugs, all different (***especially*** the one for Frond must be different).
- Decaf or some adequate substitute [initially offstage]. Don't put too much in each of the mugs -- just enough to make it look as if she poured some for each of the panellists.
- [Death scene] Frond's calendar

Andy Johnson
- travel receipts
- itemized list of expenses
- vial of poison

Ruthie Westover
- large purse with maybe a dozen butterscotch and other puddings in it. Also a set of handcuffs.

Frond
- Note card for opening introductions and remarks
- bruise makeup for death scene [off stage]
- blood to apply to corner of mouth [also done off stage]

Bobbitt
- cellphone (uses it twice)

Robin Bobbitt, Ruthie, and Andy: possibly business cards

General
- Possibly salmon or tuna juice for death scene.

Shrink-Wrapped Murder

Scene 1

*[**Frond** and the three other panellists (**Bobbitt, Westover, and Johnson**) have found seats among the audience and are sitting as the scene opens.*

Frond stands as Phillipa yells at him and remains standing. The other three stand when introduced but then sit down again.]

Phillipa [**Screams** *outside the room, probably with door open into room so audience can hear clearly,* then shouts "**How could you?**" *with continued exasperated utterances as she enters, yelling to Frond from across the room]*

[***Frond** stands*]

Dr. Frond! I'm very sorry, but the incompetent staff at this place have forgotten to provide computer projection services for our panel presentations after dinner.

Frond That's something you should have prepared for, Phillipa. Tell them they have an hour while we're eating dinner to arrange the necessary equipment.

Phillipa Yes, sir. *[exits]*

Frond Ladies and Gentlemen and fellow students of life, thank you for coming this evening... I am Dr. Sigmoid Frond, Chair of the Department of Human Behaviour at the City University of New Trent.

We have a very interesting after-dinner symposium prepared for you this evening, bringing together some of the world's top psychologists. The speakers will include ... [*Looks at note card*] Dr. Robin Bobbitt, a well known television therapist. [*Indicates Bobbitt, who stands. Frond waits for applause*]. Dr. Bobbitt hasn't really done any research of academic standing on human behaviour, but he brings a wealth of experience to the symposium.

Bobbitt   My research is impeccable, as you well know, Dr. Frond, based on my counselling experiences. I will be happy to share it with everyone this evening. [*sits*]

Frond   Next we have Dr. Ruth Westover [*indicates Westover, who stands. Frond waits for applause*]. Dr. Westover has used some quite unorthodox research methods to arrive at conclusions that are certainly at variance with my own **seminal** results, which, I might add, are the accepted standard in the profession, meaning that hers are undoubtedly flawed in some manner. But we'll save that discussion for the actual symposium.

Westover   We'll talk more soon, Dr. Frond. [*sits*]

Frond   And our third panellist is the esteemed Dr. Andy Johnson. [*indicates Johnson, who stands. Frond waits for applause*]. Dr. Johnson has spent years in the South Pacific and in Vancouver Canada studying the group dynamics of the Buhu gangs. He has made his name using flowcharts to demonstrate the group dynamics he has identified.

Johnson   Thank you, Dr. Frond, and if it will help, I don't really need the projector for my presentation. I can just use an easel to sketch the various communal links we identified among the Buhu.

Frond   Thank you, Dr. Johnson, but it would greatly enhance your presentation, and especially your corroboration of my own research, which of course pre-dated yours, if we could all see your computer graphic presentation.

Johnson   That's okay, Dr. Frond. I'm sure I'll be able to ... [*sits after being interrupted by Westover*]

Westover   [*Interrupts sarcastically*]. Which earlier work of yours were you referring to, Sigmoid? Was it "Sex and the Lizard" that you wrote back in 1974? Or are you referring to your 1975 article, "Freud and The Kama Sutra"?

Phillipa   [*returns during end of Ruthie's questions*]

Frond   [*Ignores Ruthie's pointed questions but turns angrily to Phillipa (as if it's her fault he hasn't written anything of importance in the past 40 years)*] Well, Phillipa, what arrangements have you made for the computer projector?

Phillipa The hotel staff say they have a connections with both Staples and Kinky's.... [*Embarrassed pause*]...Kinkos and will have something here by the end of dinner.

[*Acting innocent but getting a dig in at Frond*]: But will anyone really need a projector, Dr. Frond?

Frond [*impatiently interrupting her*] Phillipa, you know very well that I shall need a computer projection system for my Power Point slide show demonstrating how all recent developments in psychology are based on my seminal research from 30 years ago. Go back and make sure they are able to get the equipment here on time. One hour! ... And bring me a cup of decaf when you come back!

[*Phillipa exits, then returns with de-caf coffee in heavy mug for Frond after a few minutes*]

Scene Two

[AUDIENCE CARD #1:
Go up to Dr. Bobbitt. Tell him how pleased you are to meet him finally in person. Then explain that you were the person who phoned his television show last week to ask whether chocolate pudding or whipped cream was better. When you are asked what you were using chocolate pudding and whipped cream for, hesitate, act puzzled and then tell him "Well, dessert of course!".

Bobbitt Yes, Your call puzzled me. I've been wondering... Just how were you using the chocolate pudding and whipped cream? What were you using them for?

[AUD #1] .... Well, dessert of course!

Bobbitt Really? I wonder what the main course was... [Turns with a slight leer toward Ruthie] Ruthie, I can't remember which it was that you enjoyed using ... as you advanced your career.... Was it butterscotch or chocolate pudding?

Westover I think you're letting yourself get swept away by your own fantasies again, Rob Bob.

Bobbitt I don't think so, Ruthie. And you know very well my name is Robin Bobbitt, not Rob Bob. But seriously, which do you prefer: butterscotch or chocolate pudding? I can't remember.

Westover Why are you so interested in puddings, Robbie Bobbie? Do you need a little something extra to add some excitement to your real life? Or is it because you need a research topic to justify that phony PhD you've been using to call yourself "doctor"?

Bobbitt *[Indignantly]* After you and I spent some time together a few years ago, I earned a legitimate doctor's degree from The University of the Internet. And....

Westover [*interrupting*] The University of the Internet??? *[Peals of laughter]*

Bobbitt *[defensively]* Yes, they gave me credit for my work counselling people on my television program. You should have considered them. Then you wouldn't have had to sleep with all your professors and research subjects to get your own degrees.

Westover That was legitimate research, Robbie Bobbie. I was doing very important research on fantasies and motivations. In fact, just tonight [**...AUD MEMBER...**] here asked if s/he can be my next subject.... Sorry, [**AUD**] but I have a very looonnnnngggg waiting list.

Phillipa, could you get me a cup of that decaf coffee, too?

Bobbitt I think I'd like a cup of decaf, as well, Phillipa. [*glaring at Ruthie*] There seems to be a bit of a chill in here.

Frond Phillipa, why don't you just bring some decaf for each of the panellists? And bring something for yourself, too. ***[Phillipa exits]***

And by the way, Dr. Bobbitt, to answer your earlier question: Dr. Westover has used a great deal of butterscotch pudding in her research. Actually, I was privileged enough to have her demonstrate its use for me – very tasty, especially the way she employs it in her taste tests...

*[**Phillipa** returns in a few minutes with a tray of four mugs of coffee similar to (but distinguishable from) the one she brought Frond earlier. She distributes them to the other three, lingering very admiringly and gushing over Andy Johnson. All coffee mugs must be heavy and distinguishable from Dr. Frond's mug.]*

[During the upcoming scene break, Johnson tries to chat up Westover unsuccessfully. He keeps trying throughout the night. Some audience members might hear him mention his extensive collection of the music by Hootie and the Blowfish.]

Scene Three

[**Audience Card #2:** Go up to Dr. Johnson and ask him if he has done any research on the anxiety that arises from sibling rivalry.

Johnson Actually, I spent several years studying precisely this problem among the Buhu gang in Vancouver. We came up with several possible cures for sibling rivalry anxiety. The most effective treatment was scream therapy. Phillipa, you let out a good scream earlier this evening. Maybe you could come over here to help this person.

[*To **AUD #2**:*] You try first – scream as loud and high-pitched as you can.

That's pretty good. [*or if not, ask Aud to do it again*]. Now, Phillipa, you scream as loud and high-pitched as you can.

Phillipa *[screams]*

Johnson Excellent. Now the two of you scream together, right at each other, looking right in each other's eyes.

[*Gets them to repeat, both alternating screams and screaming in unison*]

That's how it works, [*To **AUD #2***] and you are off to a pretty good start. Probably all you need to do is find a partner who will help satisfy your needs...to scream, that is.

AUD #2: Oh, I wasn't asking for myself. It was for my mother…

Johnson [*To Frond*]: Dr. Frond, were you able to deal with my request that you serve Fugu [*pronounced FOO-goo*] for dinner this evening? I have enjoyed the delicacy several times. Were you able to locate anyone around here who can provide it for this evening's meal? Especially someone who can prepare it safely and properly?

Frond I realize you have a strong addiction to BLOWfish like the Fugu. [*smirk*]. But, no, we won't be serving any Fugu tonight. Speaking of BLOWfish and addictions, have things been resolved with those ethical questions about your research with those young men in Vancouver?

Johnson I have no idea what you're talking about. All that happened was that one of the mothers overheard me talking about the sects in the Buhu gang … Sect..sss. S-E-C-T-S. She misheard what I said and thought I was promoting gang sex.

Frond Remember, Dr. Johnson, I took you under my wing only because your research results could be adjusted to confirm the results of my own seminal work. Don't forget everything I've done for you.

*[**Crucial**: At this point Frond must set his coffee mug down somewhere out of the way, where audience members are unlikely to watch it. A windowsill or serving table or maybe one end of the bar will do]*

Scene 4

[**Audience card #3**. Go up to Dr. Frond and tell him you've had some very interesting dreams recently. Ask him if he can help you understand them. He will ask you to tell him about a recent dream. Tell him you dreamed you were standing in a rowboat in the middle of a very calm lake when suddenly a large claw emerged from the water to try to grab you.. When he asks "Was this at night or during the day?" indignantly tell him "It was at night! I don't sleep on the job!"

*[**Crucial**: During the dream discussion, Johnson wanders to Frond's cup and hovers over it briefly but unnoticed.]*

Frond And what was your dream about?
[*Wait for answer; draw out details if possible, muttering "I see, I see" after each answer. E.g. what were you wearing? How big was the lake? What colour was the claw? Were you perfectly erect in the rowboat?*]
Ah, a classical Freudian dream scenario. Was this at night or during the day? [**AUD:** at night. I don't sleep on the job!]
I mean *within* your dream itself. Did it take place at night or during the day?
[*wait for answer but then continue regardless of the answer*]. I see. Well, in standard dream analysis, water represents a strong sexual desire, and the fact that you were standing in a rowboat suggests you were trying to avoid having sex but were afraid of being trapped or clawed back into the deep dark waters of sexual desires. As I said, it's a classical Freudian dream for people who are either sexually repressed or who are trying to stand, erect above the darker sides of sexual behaviour. Be sure to talk that over with your partner soon! Now, where did I put my coffee? [*Frond retrieves coffee mug from wherever he may have left it and sips from it.*] [*to* **AUD**] If you would like to explore the subject more, I'll be happy to take you on as a private client. Phillipa, be sure to get this person's name and phone number and make an appointment for next week.

Phillipa Of course, Dr. Frond, but before I do, may I ask: is *every* dream related to sex?

Frond Phillipa, you have been with me long enough to know that everything in life is about sex. Even that clipboard and pen you carry around are important sex symbols, especially the way you push so hard on that pen when you are writing. From now on, don't embarrass yourself by asking me questions here.

Phillipa But Dr. Frond, you've told me not to talk when we're alone together...

Frond Then use your pen and notepad and write out your questions!

[*Phillipa begins scribbling furiously, tears off a sheet of paper, and hands it to Frond. Frond looks at it and stuffs it into his pocket. The note says, "Why do you like butterscotch pudding so much when we're together?" this note will be retrieved from his pocket later.*]

Frond None of your business. We'll discuss this later.

Phillipa But how? You don't want to discuss anything with me when we're alone. All you ever want to do is…

Frond [*hurriedly interrupting Phillipa*]. Fine, we'll talk the next time. Okay??

Phillipa Okay [goes to **Aud #3** to collect information for a possible appointment with Frond.]

Scene 5

[*During this scene and the next, Frond begins slurring his words and stumbling VERY imperceptibly at first, building VERY slowly over time. At first it will appear to be inconsequential. And by the time Scene 6 ends, it will still not be flagrant or overly obvious, just noticeable to some. Hint: act slightly drunk. Do NOT be too obvious but make sure people will be able to recall and refer to the incidents later*].

Westover [*Flirty tone*] Dr. Frond, my promotion should be up for review this year but it seems to have been delayed for some reason. Based on my entire body [*slight pose*]…of work I think I should be promoted this year, not next. Wouldn't you agree?

Frond Indeed your work has been excellent to date Dr. Westover. All the members of the promotion committee have been very impressed especially with your contributions to the … um…oral traditions of psychology.

Westover I'm confident I can continue my work with you and maybe even do some work with the other members of the committee as well.

Frond Um, well, yes, I suppose so but be sure you don't ignore the continuing work that you and I have been conducting on the Freudian implications of touching and feeling… [*Stumbles slightly*]

Westover [*overly effusive, bordering on sarcasm but still flirty*] Of course Dr. Frond.

Bobbitt Speaking of collaboration, Dr. Frond, I have sent of number of patients your way from my television show "Round Pegs, Round Holes". I thought we had an agreement that I would receive a referral fee from you for each patient I sent your way.

Frond Yes, well they didn't all make appointments, and those who did make appointments didn't all show up.

Bobbitt But still some did show up, right?

Frond Well, yes, but most of those people chose not to continue their treatment after the initial visit. I don't owe you a referral fee if they didn't actually become patients.

Bobbitt Yes, you do. You owe me a small referral fee for every patient you've seen, plus a larger fee for those you continued to treat. That was our agreement. I haven't seen a penny of it.

Frond Do you have a copy of that agreement?

Bobbitt Of course not. I trusted you. You owe me for those referrals.

Frond Well, come see me tomorrow and we'll settle up.

Scene 6 *[near the end of dinner]*

Johnson Excuse me Dr. Frond. Excuse me.

Frond [*impatiently*] Yes, yes. What is it Johnson?

Johnson I have my travel expenses here for coming to this symposium. You said you would cover them for me?

Frond [*Still impatiently*] Yes, yes. Just see Phillipa and give her the itemized list and travel receipts. She looks after the administrative matters…

Johnson [*looking around, finds Phillipa*] Oh yes. Um. Phillipa?

Phillipa [*almost gushing*] Yes, Dr. Johnson?

Johnson Please. Call me Andy.

Phillipa Okay, Andyyy....

Johnson Sigmoid said he would cover my expenses for this trip, but from what I've heard tonight, I'm concerned. Do you think you can look after these expenses for me?

Phillipa *[flirty]* Of course... Andy. *[Takes receipts and itemized list, adding them to her clipboard]*

Johnson Thanks. *[Returns his attention to Frond]*
Dr. Frond, I'd also like to meet with you tomorrow, if possible, to talk about your misrepresentation of my work. I know you said that my research on group dynamics among the Buhu sects has a Freudian basis related to your own research, but I don't think that is correct. I was studying sects, not sex. *[trying very hard to enunciate the difference clearly]*.

Frond Yes, yes. Make an appointment with Phillipa. But if you'll sssscuse me, right now I think I need to use the Gents. I'll be back in a few minutes. **[*exits staggering slightly*]**.

Johnson *[as Frond exits]* Certainly. ... um...Thank you.

[To Phillipa] Excuse me Phillipa. I'm sure you heard that exchange. Can you make an appointment for me to speak with Dr. Frond tomorrow sometime? I'm not returning to Lichtenstein until the day after tomorrow.

Phillipa My appointment calendar for Dr. Frond is in my car, Andy. How about I take you out for a drink after the symposium and we can work on it then?

Johnson Oh, well, ... *[looks at Westover longingly]* ... I'm not sure. I might be busy. Maybe you can email a time for me when you have a chance?

Phillipa *[Disappointed]* Of course. Why don't I just go get the calendar from my car now so we can settle on a time before the panel presentations begin. **[*exits*]**.

Bobbitt [*puts hand to pocket containing cellphone. Takes out phone and looks at it.*] Excuse me, please. My cellphone is buzzing, and I need to take this call. I'll just step outside. [***exits***]

Johnson Ruthie, I've been hoping for a chance to speak with you.

Bobbitt Not now, Andy. Not here.

Johnson But you know I want to see more of you. When? Where?

Bobbitt [*exasperated*] aahhhggg. [*storms of out room*].

Johnson But Ruthie! I thought we clicked that weekend in Hamilton. [*Pass out Audience card #4 after delivering this line. Then musing out loud to crowd*]. Hmmm. I wonder what's taking Dr. Frond so long.

[**Audience Card #4**] He went to the men's room. What do you **think** is taking him so long? Duh!

Johnson Well, I'd better go check on him to see if he's okay.

Scene 7 [Death and accusations] *[after dinner]*

[*During the break:*
- *Bruise on Frond's forehead.*
- *Blood dripping from corner of Frond's mouth.*
- *Note from Phillipa in Frond's pocket (should still be there).*
- *Phillipa has notepad, pen, Frond's calendar, and Johnson's itemized travel expenses.*
- *Frond's necktie is loosened and moved outside his collar and over his shoulder, off to one side, and hanging outside his suit/sport coat.*]

Frond bangs against the door on the way in as he staggers in and collapses. He lies there on his back, face up, unguarded but only briefly.

Phillipa [*bustling in only a few seconds after Frond "dies". Stops suddenly when she sees Frond on the floor*] [**Screams**] Oh no! What's happened, Dr. Frond? [*She bends down to check his pulse*] There's no pulse! Oh no! What happened??? [*She asks several nearby Audience members what they saw.*]

Bobbitt [*entering after Phillipa has talked with a couple of audience members and seeing Frond on the floor*]. Oh, for Pete's Sake, Sigmoid, get up. Are you **drunk, again**? [*Emphasize "drunk, again" to make it look as if he was drunk, leading to his earlier behaviour*] Sheesh.

Phillipa [*angry*] NO! He collapsed and he doesn't have a pulse. Give him mouth-to-mouth, Robin. I hear you're VERY good at that...

Johnson [*entering but speaking before seeing Frond on the floor*] Is Frond okay? He wasn't in the men's room, but there was some blood on the washbasin. [*Seeing Frond*]. Oh my goodness! What's wrong?

Phillipa He staggered in here and collapsed. I think he's dead. He doesn't have a pulse. Oh Andy, what are we going to do? I need you to help me! Please!!....

Johnson [*shrugs off Phillipa*]. Is there a doctor in the house?

Phillipa Andy, you're all doctors, aren't you?

Johnson I mean, is there a **real** doctor in the house? Not just a PhD doctor.

[*Robin passes out Audience card #5*]

Audience Card. #5 I have a medical degree. Let me take a look. [*Looks at the body. Checks pulse.*] He has a contusion on his forehead, and there is blood coming from one corner of his mouth. ...Oh, and his heart isn't beating. He's dead. [*Returns to seat*]

Bobbitt [*sarcastically*] Well thank you SO much for that insight, Doctor.

Westover [*sauntering in*] What's going on? I just stepped out for a quick toke with one of the kitchen staff. I had to dodge into the kitchen to avoid Andy Johnson.

Phillipa It looks as if Dr. Frond was hit on the head. Apparently he's dead. Are you sure you were in the kitchen, Ruthie? You seemed upset with Dr. Frond about his delay of your upcoming promotion.

Westover Yes, I was in the kitchen. …. Well, actually I was out in the parking lot off the kitchen with one of the sous-chefs. And yes, I was concerned about my upcoming promotion but I have the members of the promotion committee well in hand.

Phillipa 'Members…Well in hand'. I'm sure you do.

Westover What about you, Phill MaGraw? You were clearly angry with Dr. Frond. He kept ordering you around, and he forced you to do lord-knows-what with him when you two were alone together and he wouldn't let you talk. He was obviously bothered by the note you wrote out for him earlier tonight. Andy, is that note still in his pocket?

Johnson [*Takes note from Frond's pocket*] Yes. Here it is. [*Unfolds or uncrumples it and reads it out loud.*] Phillipa wrote, "Why do you like butterscotch pudding so much when we're together?" Phillipa, what is the meaning of this?

Phillipa Nothing. Nothing at all. I was trying to throw him off balance after the argument that Ruthie and Robin had about puddings. I knew he had been spending lots of money making many unauthorized purchases from his research funds, and I wanted to threaten him to get him to pay me more and ease up on his unacceptable treatment of me, so I scribbled off the first thing I could think of.

Westover Likely story. Or maybe he was insisting on using butterscotch pudding with you in other ways [*smirk*]. You got tired of being sexually abused by him, so you hit him when you went out to your car.

Phillipa No, I didn't hit him, but Robin could have. He was upset about being cheated by Dr. Frond. I know for a fact that Dr. Frond never paid Robin anything and made thousands of dollars treating the patients Robin referred to him.

Bobbitt Hey! [*Addresses everyone*] Yes, I was upset about being cheated, but I wouldn't kill anyone for cheating me. I had already begun referring people to other psychologists.

What about you, Ruthie? You ***say*** you were in the alley for a quickie ... I mean a quick toke... with a sous-chef, but were you really? Maybe you were fed up with the sexual demands Dr. Frond was making. He was threatening to block your promotion unless you gave in.

But did you ever resist him? Ever? As a matter of fact, did you ever resist anyone who might help you get uh.. head? [*not a typo. Pronounce it this way.*] [*Looks around room as if for confirmation that Ruthie had sex with every person in the room*]

Westover Nice try Rob Bob. And what about Johnson over there? He was upset about Frond's misrepresentation of his research and afraid of being stiffed.... Not by me, for sure, but by Frond for his travel expenses.

Phillipa We all know that Dr. Frond wasn't the most likable character, and we all probably had some reason for wanting him out of our lives. But how do we even know he was murdered, anyway? Maybe he just slipped and banged his head on the washbasin?

Bobbitt I'm calling the police [*takes out cellphone and dials 911*]. Hello, I'd like to report a murder...... at ___[*performance venue*]___ . .... I see.... Well how long do you think it will be before someone can get here? ......I see... Oh, well then never mind. [*Disconnects*] They say they're busy raiding a prostitution ring in Sarnia right now and can't get here until they're finished sometime tomorrow.

Phillipa I guess since I was Dr. Frond's assistant, I'll have to take charge. So let's collect whatever evidence we can find and put it over here on this table.

Let's see there's this note that I wrote to him. And what else?

Johnson What about all that stuff you've been carrying around, Phillipa? The notepad, the pen, and Dr. Frond's calendar for sure...

Westover ...and all these coffee mugs? Maybe someone hit him in the head with a coffee mug?

Phillipa *[Eye roll]*. What*ever*. And Ruthie that purse you've been carrying looks big enough to hold all sorts of murder weapons. Let's have a look… [Westover resists]… Come on, Ruthie, hand it over. [Westover relents]

[Phillipa dumps purse onto table. The only contents are a set of handcuffs and a dozen or so boxes of dried butterscotch pudding mixes and some individual-sized containers of butterscotch puddings.]

Pudding and handcuffs! So Ruthie, always prepared to do more research, are you?

Westover What's your problem, MaGraw? Jealous??

Phillipa As I said, 'What*ever*'. The rest of you can come up and look at the evidence and examine the body **_without touching it_** .

Fill out your suggestion slips and we'll collect them in just a few minutes. Who killed Dr. Frond? How? And Why?

[Note: it might be fun if the dessert could include an option for chocolate or butterscotch pudding with whipped cream; or maybe chocolate mousse.]

Denouement

Phillipa Well, those certainly were some very interesting suggestions that you people offered for how Dr. Frond was killed. [*Fans self*] Whew! My, oh my!

Westover Oh, knock it off, MaGraw! There's nothing in those suggestions you haven't seen before. We all know you wanted Frond dead because he was pushing you around and making you do things you didn't want to do. Do you want a list? Let's start with the butterscotch pudding, shall we?

Johnson [*quickly interrupting*]. Leave her alone Ruthie. You're just plain mean and nasty, and you have used your wiles to get uh...head. But Frond was insisting on even more demonstrations of your wiles with him, wasn't he. You were tiring of it all, and you weren't sure you could trust him to follow through and support your next promotion.

Bobbitt Johnson's right, Ruthie, you are a mean, and nasty piece ... of work. You **say** you were out in the alley with a sous-chef, but we have only your word for it. He'll probably go along with whatever you say if you promise to meet him later and knowing you, that's exactly what you have already done. Right?

Westover I **was** out in the alley. And if you think I killed Frond, how do you think I did it? We don't even know **how** he was killed! Look at him!

Bobbitt No thanks.

Westover [*continuing*] His necktie isn't under his collar anymore. Someone probably moved it up and strangled him, forcing his head onto the washbasin edge. The blood around his mouth came when he resisted being strangled.

Phillipa You're just full of good ideas, aren't you Ruthie? First you say he was hit over the head with a coffee cup. Now you say he was strangled with his own necktie. Any other great ideas?

Johnson Yeah, maybe Ruthie wasn't in the alley at all. Maybe she had her way with him and he had a heart attack and fell against the washbasin and that's what caused the bleeding I saw there. ... Or maybe **she** hit him with a coffee mug but suggested that to throw suspicion away from herself...

Bobbitt That bruise on his forehead doesn't look serious enough to have come from a lethal blow. I really doubt if that's what killed him. It might have, but I think we should look for some other cause of death.

Phillipa I don't see that any of his teeth have been knocked out. Andy, did you push him against the washbasin? Is that what caused the bump on his head? Maybe that caused an injury inside his mouth that led to this bleeding?

Westover Well, I'm sure you'd know the inside of Frond's mouth well enough to know, quick-draw MaGraw.

Phillipa No better than you. Why don't you look to see? ...

Johnson I don't see any marks on his neck, ...so I really doubt if someone used his necktie to strangle him.

Bobbitt Wait a minute. Did any of you notice that Dr. Frond was beginning to slur his words ever so slightly? Maybe about twenty minutes or so before he died?

Phillipa [*surprised*] You're right, Robin. It seemed uncharacteristic of him.

Bobbitt And he stumbled or staggered just a bit a few times, too. I thought he was drunk.

Westover He certainly acted as if he was well on his way to being fully tanked.

Phillipa But that's not possible. All he had had to drink this evening was this decaf I gave him. ... [*picks up Frond's cup*]... He didn't have any alcohol to drink. ... Say, does this smell a bit fishy to you [*passes cup around to other cast members, not audience unless some tuna or salmon juice has been added at some point*].

Johnson Dr. Frond's behaviour has always seemed more than a bit fishy if you ask me, but I don't smell anything unusual about this cup.

Phillipa Well I sure do, Andy. What about you Robin and Ruthie?

Bobbitt It's not the usual kind of fishy smell I'm used to but you're right, there is some odor that doesn't seem right.

Westover I can smell it, too. ...Andy Baby, what's wrong with you that you can't smell it?

[pause. Pause. Then the light goes on for Phillipa]

Phillipa Oh no!! Andy, say it isn't true!

Johnson What? What on earth are you talking about?

Phillipa I had to do some research on FOO-goo fish for Dr. Frond because you asked us to have some available for tonight's dinner. If Fugu isn't prepared properly, parts of the fish containing tetrodotoxin can kill people. There have been numerous incidents involving poorly prepared Fugu blowfish causing people to die. It takes only a drop or two of the toxin to kill someone, and they die within about twenty minutes or so --- that fits the timeline of Dr. Frond's death!

Andy, you would have known all about Fugu and tetrodotoxin – you studied Asian sects in both Southeast Asia and Vancouver... Oh, Andy!

Johnson Yes, of course I know about the dangers of tetrodotoxin poisoning from Fugu blowfish. That was why I asked Dr. Frond to take care in finding a decent chef to prepare the delicacy for us. Besides even if I had wanted to poison his coffee, when would I have done it? Phillipa, you're the one who brought him his coffee.

Bobbitt And she just admitted that she had researched the ins and outs [...pause...] of Fugu poisoning. She'd have known how to do this!

Phillipa Now wait just a minute!! We're in [Ontario, Canada]! There are NO Fugu around here. None. You can't even get them from a fish wholesaler. I couldn't possibly have gotten my hands on the poison. *[looking sad and lost]* But Andy, you could have. You often visited with chefs in Vancouver who prepared Fugu. You could have put a few drops of the poison into Dr. Frond's cup at any time.

Westover No wonder Frond was beginning to act slightly drunk! He'd been poisoned! AndyBoy put the poison into his coffee earlier this evening.

Phillipa Remember when Dr Frond went over to the [*wherever he set it down*] to pick up his mug after he did that dream analysis? He'd left it there. Anyone could have poisoned it then.

Bobbitt And Frond wasn't feeling well as the poison began to take effect, so he loosened his tie as went to the men's room. I'm betting he stumbled against the washbasin as the poison took greater effect.

Johnson Just keep in mind that every one of these people here wanted Frond dead, and so did each of you. [*Pulls vial out of pocket and holds it up for all to see*]. I hated that man. He was seriously misrepresenting my research, and he had ruined my career in the process. I'm sure he was going to try to stiff me for my travel expenses, too. I knew when I came here that I was going to poison him, and I'm glad I did it. And be honest: you all know I did each and every one of you a favour.

But now, I think I'll try boarding an earlier flight back to Lichtenstein, before the police come to investigate. [***Exits***].

Phillipa Andy! Wait! I'd have made sure you got paid! Wait! I'll help you run away! Take me with you. Maybe we can have some Fugu together... [***Exits***]

Bobbitt [*leering at Ruthie*] Well, Ruthie, it's just you and me now, Babe.

Westover [*sneers at a leering Bobbitt*] Forget it Rob Bob. Just because we're the last two persons standing doesn't mean we're having some butterscotch pudding together tonight. [***Exits***].

Bobbitt Wait, Ruthie! What about chocolate pudding then??? With whipped cream??? [***Exits***]

The End

Possible name tags

It might be a nice touch if everyone in attendance had convention-type nametags, which would help the audience identify the major characters and help the actors remember the names of audience members. During the cocktail hour, Phillipa could go around with labels and a Sharpie to do this.

Be careful about using the nametags suggested here, though. They may not go over well with some or many audiences.

Dr. Sigmoid Frond
City University of New Trent

Dr. Ruthie Westover
Toronto Wesleyan Academy of Therapists

Dr. Robin Bobbitt
Host, "Round Pegs, Round Holes"
Psych. Educ. Network & Info Service

Dr. Andrew Johnson
Vancouver And Global Inst. of Neuro Anxiety
and
Lichtenstein Inst. for Psycho Synthesis

Phillipa MaGraw
Administrative Ass.

Audience card #1

Go up to Dr. Bobbitt and say,
Dr. Bobbit, I'm so pleased to meet you in the flesh finally. I'm the person who called you last week to ask whether chocolate pudding or whipped cream is better.

When Dr. Bobbitt asks you what you were using chocolate pudding and whipped cream for, hesitate, act puzzled and then tell him **"Well, dessert of course!"**
            DO THIS NOW! BE VERY LOUD!

Audience Card #2

Go up to Dr. Johnson and ask him,
    "Have you done any research on sibling rivalry?"

He will offer some suggestions and give you some exercises.
After he says you'll need to find a partner to help satisfy your needs, tell him, **"Oh, I wasn't asking for myself! It was for my mother."**
            DO THIS NOW! BE VERY LOUD!

Audience Card #3

Go up to Dr. Frond and say
"Dr. Frond, I have had some very interesting dreams lately. Can you help me understand them?"

He will ask you to tell him about a recent dream. Tell him:
"I dreamed I was standing in a rowboat in the middle of a very calm lake when suddenly a large claw emerged from the water to try to grab me."

When he asks "Was this at night or during the day?" indignantly tell him **"It was at night! I don't sleep on the job!"**

DO THIS NOW! BE VERY LOUD!

Audience Card #4

When Dr. Johnson asks "Hmmm. I wonder what's taking Dr. Frond so long." You should shout out...

"He went to the men's room. What do you *think* is taking him so long? Duh!"

BE VERY LOUD!!

Audience Card #5

After Dr. Johnson says, "I mean a real doctor, not a PhD doctor," stand up and say **"I have a medical degree. Let me take a look."**

Go look at the body and check his pulse. Stand up and announce, **"He has a contusion on his forehead, and there is blood coming from one corner of his mouth. ...Oh, and his heart isn't beating. He's dead."** [and then return to your seat]

**Murder weapon? Fugu? Tetrodotoxin?
http://content.time.com/time/specials/packages/article/0,28804,1967235_1967238_1967227,00.html**

Murder at the Office New Year's Eve Party

It's time for the annual New Year's Eve party at Arttekko *[ar-TECH-oh]*, a firm that produces and distributes thousands of art prints to hotels, motels, and commercial buildings every year. Betty Batchly, the CEO, inherited the firm when her husband died over a decade ago, and she has been the driving force behind Arttekko's success. She is so compelled to be successful that she angers and/or hurts everyone around her, some of whom are either not nice at all or too nice to be believed. Who dies? Who kills the victim and how? Everyone in this group of highly motivated executives has a motive. Surely someone should be able to solve the case…

By John P. Palmer
© Copyright 2019

Character Descriptions

Betty Batchly:

Betty is the CEO of Arttekko, a corporation that sells mass-produced artwork in batches of hundreds, even thousands, to hotels and corporations. She buys up the rights to photos or artwork to use for her business, but mostly she uses artwork that is no longer protected by copyright. At times, however, she has been known to use some artwork without properly acquiring the rights, and then she feigns ignorance if anyone complains.

Betty is a very driven entrepreneur. She built her business after her late husband's printing business went belly up. She says, "It went 'butt up', not 'belly up'. He fell flat on his face with his butt up in the air because he couldn't keep up with the times." Betty has a large production, warehouse, and shipping facility in a nearby small town [e.g. Thamesford] where they print the art, frame it, and ship it in lots no smaller than two dozen each. She has an extensive online catalogue to choose from, and her prices are very low because she standardized her prints to only four different sizes. But she is facing increasing threats of competition from firms in Asia or from North American firms that produce the art in Asia and ship it from there.

Betty is honest but tough. She is so driven that she seems cruel and heartless. She is late 40s - early 60s, sharp mentally, and sharp-tongued. At one time or another, she has clearly antagonized everyone who has ever worked with or for her.

[Victim]

...

Tim Jones:

Tim is a business school product who thinks he knows more than he does and thinks he is more capable than he is. He keeps telling people that he knows the company could make more money if only they would [import more work from Asia; or use 3-D printers to print the artwork and the frames all in one piece; or spend more money on wining and dining hotel and office building executives; or hold more exhibitions for the hotel and resort business managers, etc.].

Tim is macho, slick, and ambitious. He fully anticipates he will be made Vice President of Arttekko within the next year or sooner and has his eye on Betty's job as President. Failing that he's sure he will have no problem finding an executive position elsewhere. As the evening wears on, it becomes clear that Betty has no interest in promoting him. He is furious and makes vague threats that people would ordinarily believe are made only in the heat of the moment. Age range: early 30s to early 50s. Tim is married (to **AUD #3** from the audience).
   [Motive: upset at not being promoted faster]

David Dekker:

David was hired by Betty's late husband and has been with the firm since long before Betty expanded it from merely being a printing shop into a global art supplier. He is mild-mannered, meek, kind, and helpful. He looks after the mail, the coffee, the stockroom, etc. He is generally a suck-up gofer. Elizabeth is smarter and more ambitious than David, but she is drawn to his kind personality. He loves looking after Elizabeth and doesn't like the fact that Betty seems not to appreciate her. Also David doesn't like the fact that Tim seems to be outmaneuvering Elizabeth in the game of corporate politics. Betty and Tim think David is a wimp and treat him that way. Age range 40s to late 50s. Also passive-aggressive.
[Motive: resents Betty's treatment of both Elizabeth and himself]

Elizabeth Hurd:

Elizabeth is a hard-working, mildly ambitious senior manager at Arttekko. She and Tim compete to show who is better, smarter, and kinder when kindness is called for. She's a bit of a geek. She resents and is even jealous of Tim's veneer of confidence, and she knows she should have more authority and decision-making power in the firm than she does. She defers to Tim but makes very negative, snide remarks about him when he isn't around. She is very clearly passive-aggressive.

Elizabeth has had an ongoing secret relationship with the older David, the long-time stockboy/mailroom/gofer for the firm. They have matching rings that they wear on their right hands "Oh these? Just a coincidence I guess."

Elizabeth received her business training at the local for-profit college, Thames College. She knows the training wasn't very good, but she also has finally realized she has more smarts and ability than Tim. Age 30s – 50s

[Motive: she knows she deserves more recognition for her abilities; she resents that both she and David are being put down all the time.]

Geraldine [or Geri] Elliot:

Geri is the somewhat shady major purchasing agent for the global letoM Motel chain. She spends hundreds of thousands of dollars on art for her motel chain each year, and in that capacity, she controls the purchasing decisions of one of the largest customers for Arttekko. Betty knows that Geri pads her expenses and takes kickbacks from the suppliers; Betty has evidence of this. Geri's job will be in jeopardy if Betty blows the whistle on her. So long as letoM Motels keep buying art from Arttekko, Betty won't do that, but the stress and worry are getting Geri down. Married to **AUD#2.** Age range open.

[Motive: afraid that Betty will tell letoM about bribes and expense-account padding]

Costumes

Generally, the costumes should be fancy party type garb. David wears a white shirt and tie; he starts with a sportcoat (purportedly covering the gun he has tucked in his waistband at the back, but don't put it there until Scene 4).

Guests should be encouraged to dress in festive costumes themselves: Sweaters from Christmas, left-over mistletoe and other Christmas headbands, etc.

Murder at the Office New Year's Eve Party

Scene 1

*There must be a table or suitable space to put the New Year's poster and fruitcake. David will bring in the poster during **this** scene and will bring in the cake and knife later.*

Before the show begins,
David *selects a table and designates four of the people at that table to be the singers known as "The Artichokes", rehearses them briefly, and shows them the dance moves for Winter Wonderland.*
Tim*, and* ***Geri****, should select appropriate audience members to be their spouses,* ***Elizabeth*** *should stake out two places to sit – one for herself and one for David, even though he won't be using it, and*
David *should interact with the audience, but he should leave the room before the scene begins.]*

Betty: Good evening, everyone, and welcome to the annual Arttekko New Year's Eve party. We're so glad you could all be here to celebrate our continued success. We know **we** wouldn't be here if it weren't for all of **you!**

Later this evening, as we are concluding dinner, we will have our traditional ceremony where we light up the poster to welcome in the New Year. At that time, we will dim the room lights and **then**, just as we turn on the lights around the poster, we will all pop our poppers and blow into our noise makers *[points, indicating toy horns and other noise makers]*. So even though it's tempting to pull a popper or blow something right now, please wait until we give you the go ahead.

David: *[Entering with poster; garland and lights already on it.]* Excuse me, Ms. Batchly, here's the New Year's Eve poster with the lights and garland already on it. Should I put it here on the table?

Betty: *[tersely]* That'll be fine, David. Did you test the lights to make sure they work?

David: Yes, I did, Ms. Batchly. Here, I'll show you *[moves to turn on the lights]*.

Betty: *[shouts]* **NO!!!** Don't turn them on yet, not in here. You know I don't want them turned on until the proper time!

David: *[meekly]* Yes, Ma'am.

Elizabeth: David, I've saved a place for you to sit over here with me.

David: Thanks, Elizabeth, I'd like that, but I already have a place over there with the company choir, the Artichokes.

Elizabeth: Okay. Well, when you're finished there with the poster could you please bring me a drink?

David: Sure. *[Bustles around the poster a bit, then gets drinks for Elizabeth and Tim (see below)].*

Tim: *[sarcastically]* He's such a good helper. More like a mascot for Arttekko than an employee. And just about as productive. Hey, David, bring me a drink, too, will ya?

Elizabeth: Stop that, Tim! David does lots of things for everyone here at Arttekko.

Betty: *[sternly]*. You two! This is supposed to be a party, not a snipe session. *[To audience]*... And one of the reasons we can keep partying and being successful as a firm involves our close working relationship with the worldwide chain of letoM *[pronounced 'Let 'em']* Motels. LetoM Motels knows they can count on Arttekko to deliver appropriate artwork for all their interiors, on time, and error-free. And here from letoM Motels to help us ring in the New Year is our primary letoM contact Geri Eliot. *[Leads applause]*

Geri: Thank you, Betty. And thanks for inviting me. The relationship between LetoM and Arttekko is a two-way street. We all benefit from it in many ways.

Betty: Thanks, Geri. *[to room]* As you all know, my late husband Norman Batchly started our firm nearly forty years ago when he bought Kelly Printing. Without Norman's early efforts we all wouldn't be here today, celebrating at our annual New Year's Eve party. So please join me in a toast, to Norman. *[Raises glass]*

Others: *[loudly]* To Norman.

David: *[sneezes into clean handkerchief and blows nose.]*

Elizabeth: Bless you.

David: Thanks, Elizabeth.

Betty: *[interrupting]* And now let's also keep in mind that it was only because of our expansion into the mass-produced art business that we have all thrived as Kelly Printing evolved and grew into Arttekko. To Arttekko.

Others: *[loudly]* To Arttekko.

Scene 2

[Audience Card #1]
Go up to Geri Eliot of letoM Motels and ask, "Geri Eliot, How did LetoM get its name?"

Geri: Perhaps you've already figured out that "LetoM" *[says the letters separately]* ...L...E...T...O...M is just "motel" spelled backwards. The founder of the chain thought of the name so that when he put neon lights on top of the motels, the signs would say "letoM Motel" from either direction.

But when people started making jokes about, "What does 'motel' say backwards?" we captured an entire market of people who thought a motel named "Let 'em" would rent rooms by the hour.

*[To **AUD #1**]* Have you ever stayed at one of our motels? *[Wait for answer; and whatever they answer, continue "and why not?" or "what did you think of it?"]*

Tim: Hey Geri, it's good to see you again. Too bad things didn't work out for us to spend more time together at the trade show in Las Vegas last year. I was hoping maybe we could *[leer]*, you know, 'go bowling' together, but here you are now…

Geri: *[interrupting]* I was at the trade show on business, Tim, and I'm here on business, too. So just cool it, will you?

Betty: *[Glares at Tim; then speaks to Geri]* And we're glad to have you here, too, Geri. Thanks again for coming.
But I did want to ask you about something, Geri. I've been sending you "finder's fees" for the past six years to thank you for finding us and directing all of LetoM's business our way. But I got a notice last month from LetoM's head office that they do not charge finders' fees and that we are not to pay any person or agent a finders' fee.

Geri: Yeah, well….

Betty: So does this mean you've been cheating your bosses by extorting a payoff from us and from your other suppliers?

Geri: It's not extortion. It is a finders' fee --- a fee you've been very happy to pay and that you'll keep paying if you want to keep our business.

Betty: *[threateningly].* Maybe we should talk about this some more, Geri. Maybe letoM doesn't want to keep employees around who are extracting bribes from their suppliers. Maybe letoM would deeply appreciate my letting them know about your shady practices. Maybe they would show their gratitude by giving Arttekko a long-term contract. And maybe as a result, you would be blackballed in the industry. And so maybe we need to renegotiate your finder's fee, Geri.

Geri: Maybe. But then again maybe not. Let's not forget that you were eager to pay these finder's fees to get our business; you're as culpable as we are. And then there was all the flirting you did with my husband *[a pre-selected audience member]* two years ago, right **[call Audience #2 by name]**? *[Give Aud #2 card to read].*

Audience Card #2
Let's not be hasty, Geri. She was just checking to see if I had any loose change in my pockets. … And later, that position we were in? Remember we were playing Twister. It wasn't what it looked like.

Geri: Right.... And I'm supposed to believe that? Especially about a woman who bribes purchasing agents and who would do anything to grow her business? Well just don't be letting her grow **your** business if you know what's good for you.

David: *[sneezes into handkerchief again, blows nose again; exits]*

<u>**Scene 3**</u>

David: *[entering from outside the room, wiping nose]* Excuse me, Ms. Batchly, but you've received a fax.

Betty: *[impatiently]* Give it to Elizabeth. You know she looks after all our communications.

David: Yes, Ma'am. .... *[to Elizabeth]* Here, Elizabeth. *[David gazes overly-obviously and lovingly into her eyes as he hands her the telegraph.]*

Elizabeth: Thank you, David. Happy New Year. *[kisses him on his cheek]* You do so much around here.

David: Thanks, Elizabeth. *[Perhaps touches her arm lovingly and shuffles off].*

Elizabeth: Oh!! Ms. Batchly this looks important. I think you should read it now.

Betty: Read it out aloud. We have no secrets.

Elizabeth: Okaayyyy *[reluctant]*. It's from the purchasing agent of Redner Hotels. He says they have a quote from a foreign supplier to do the artwork for 30% less than we are charging.

Betty: That's nothing new. We'll deal with it in the morning. The main thing is that all our customers get exactly what they want from us in a matter of days, and they know the quality of our product. They also know we will deal with any problems immediately. And *[glaring at various members of the audience]* everyone working for Arttekko knows that heads will roll if things go wrong.

Geri: 30% lower prices? I'll have to call Redner to see what that's about?

Betty: You do that...and see what happens to your career in this business. *[to the rest of the room]* None of this foreign competition will have much effect on us or on your jobs ... yet... Those companies take three months to deliver their artwork, and if there are problems.... Well, it takes another six months to resolve anything with those firms. We're much better situated to provide speedy and high-quality service. *[To Geri]* And you know it!

Tim: But Betty, the foreign production costs are so low. I wonder if maybe we should consider shifting some of our own larger-scale production there...

Betty: Tim, I know you have a business degree, but that doesn't mean you know enough to make these decisions. Not yet. *[Sighs.]* Next week we can take **another** look at all the costs involved if you insist, but I'm sure you're wrong.

Tim: But using foreign production companies is the wave of the future, Betty. I'm sure that after I'm promoted to Vice President, as we discussed when I was hired, we will want to re-open this issue.

Betty: *[cautiously]* Yes, Tim, when we hired you, we did talk about the upside potential for you here at Arttekko. I think it's probably still there, but just not yet.

Tim: Not yet!!??? What does that mean? If not now, when?

Betty: You need to mature into the job, Tim. But here at the New Year's Eve party isn't the time or place to discuss this.

Tim: Okay, but don't expect a person with my abilities to wait too long.... *[A veiled threat; sulks and takes seat, muttering to those around him.]*

David *[David collects The Artichokes and Tim at the end of Scene 3 and takes them out to prepare costumes and to rehearse.]*

Scene 4

*[Before entering, **David** places gun in back of his waistband.]*

Betty: *[Not entirely enthusiastic]* And now, for our evening's entertainment, here is the Arttekko company choir --- "The Artichokes"!

David *[leads Artichokes in, all carrying top hats behind their backs and wearing Christmas scarves and dark glasses. All are carrying and gently ringing very small and quiet-ish sleigh bells.]*

*David is in the middle, conducting and leading the dance steps as The Artichokes sing and dance. David must **not** turn his back to the audience during the song:*

Sleigh bells ring, *[left foot out and back]* are you listening *[left foot out and back]*
In the lane, *[right foot out and back]* snow is glistening *[right foot out and back]*
A beautiful sight *[empty hand up above eyes, as if peering]*
We're happy tonight *[big smiles]*
Walking in a winter wonderland *[walking in place]*

Gone away *[left foot out and back]* is the bluebird *[left foot out and back]*
Here to stay *[right foot out and back]* is a new bird *[right foot out and back]*
He sings a love song *[empty hand over heart]*
As we go along
Walking in a winter wonderland *[walking in place]*

*[The Artichokes put on hats, then **Tim** puts a carrot in **David**'s mouth]*

> In the meadow we can build a snowman
> And pretend that he is Parson Brown
> He'll say, Are you married?
> We'll say, No man

David *[Removes carrot from his mouth and stops The Artichokes (and stops the audience if they are singing along). When they are quiet, David continues (speaking or singing the line here)]* That last line we sang was "He'll say, 'Are you married? We'll say, No man.'"

Take it, Tim!

Tim: *[sings or speaks, depending on actor's comfort zone]*
Cuz all we want to do is fool around…

David: Everyone now *[same dance steps]*:

> Later on, we'll perspire
> As we dream by the fire
> To face unafraid *[hands cup each side of face]*
> The plans that we've made
> Walking in a winter wonderland

Elizabeth: *[leads the applause but then stops abruptly, shouting as David starts to lead the choir out of the room].* **David!! I can see that gun! Did you have to bring it here? Tonight?**

David: *[pulls gun from the back of his waistband].* I carry it everywhere, Elizabeth; you know that. I always want to be prepared in case a mass shooter tries to take out a large group of people.

Elizabeth: I know, David, and I'm glad you're around, ready to protect us all, but this is New Year's Eve, David.

David: What better time for a mass shooter to attack? I think everyone here can relax just a bit knowing that I'm here with a gun.

Elizabeth: Well, maybe… *[David exits with The Artichokes to put props away. Tim and David "forget" to leave scarves with the rest of the props and are wearing them for the next few scenes.]*

Scene 5

[After The Artichokes return to the room]

Betty: Thank you again Artichokes. *[Leads applause **un**excitedly]* Good work, David. It's good to see you can do **something** right around here.

Elizabeth: What do you mean, Ms. Batchly? David does a lot of things right around here. So do all of us!

Betty: Maybe, but there are also several things that don't get done right around here, too. If Arttekko is going to survive the onslaught from its competition, we're all going to have to work harder and more carefully. Right? *[glaring at audience]* Or do you all want your jobs out-sourced to foreign producers right now?

Others: *[grumbling randomly]* Right, yes Ms. Batchly, uh huh, if you say so.

Betty: And while we're on the topic of getting things right, Elizabeth, the sales projection figures you produced for us last month were off by ten percent. Our profit margins are very thin, and we need to schedule production carefully so that we don't end up paying all these yahoos *[gestures to the audience]* for just standing around. Your errors led to some serious cost over-runs for Arttekko, Elizabeth. You'll have to do better.

Elizabeth: I know, Ms. Batchly. But the sales projection figures for the entire North American industry were off by even more than 10% last month. My predictions were better than most…

Tim: Remember what Yogi Berra said, "It's really hard to predict, especially about the future."

Betty: Be quiet, Tim. We can do without your little attempts at humour. Missing sales forecasts is a serious problem. You would know that if you paid more attention to your own work at Arttekko.

Elizabeth, this past month, you estimated the sales would be lower than they were, and to make sure we got the artwork produced and shipped out on time, Arttekko had to hire a bunch of these bozos here to work overtime and on weekends. That was **very** costly!

Elizabeth: I know, Ms. Batchly, I'm doing everything I can to narrow the margins for error.

Geri: What's the problem, Elizabeth? You know our orders from letoM Motels well in advance. Aren't all the contracts negotiated well ahead of production time?

Elizabeth: Of course they are! But last month we had a huge rush order from Trump Hotels. Given their reputation for not paying bills, we delayed work on the order until we had an 80% deposit. It took a lot of time to squeeze the deposit out of those misers, and by the time we got the deposit, we had to rush the production to meet the deadline for delivery.

Tim: *[almost creepily]* I think you've done pretty well with the forecasts, Elizabeth, but let me know if you ever want to stay late to work on them a bit more together.

Betty: Tim! If you're interested in staying late to work on things here at Arttekko, you should consider working harder and longer on your own assignments.

Audience #3 [Tim's wife stands and shrieks]

What? You mean Tim **hasn't** been working late every night this past month as he said? Tim, you scoundrel! You've been out ... bowling again, haven't you! You dirty donkey! You promised you wouldn't do that anymore ......*[pause, smile flirtatiously]*.... not without taking me along. *[She and Tim laugh together].*

[David exits sometime before next scene]

Scene 6

David: *[brings in frosted fruitcake, along with a knife, rum, and cigarette lighter; approaches Betty]* Excuse me Ms. Batchly. Here's the fruitcake that we always have after we light up the New Year's Eve poster. I have the knife here for cutting it, plenty of rum, and a cigarette lighter so we can light up the rum to flambé all the pieces as they're cut. Where should I put all these things?

Betty: *[Impatiently].* It doesn't matter. Just put them somewhere handy.

David: Yes, Ma'am. I'll put them on the table next to the poster, okay?

Betty: *[Sticks her finger in the frosting and then licks her finger.]* Eww. That frosting tastes even worse this year than it did last year. Find a better supplier next year, David.

Elizabeth: Ms. Batchly, do you think that maybe in the spirit of fresh starts for the New Year, you could show a bit more love and kindness tonight?

Betty: Love, schmove. That's no way to run a business.

Tim: Speaking of love, Elizabeth….

Elizabeth: Forget it, Tim! Don't be such a creep. And don't even think of coming near me to get a New Year's Eve kiss.

Tim: Relax, Elizabeth. When I said "speaking of love", I meant that I've noticed you and David have matching rings and that you two stand up for each other all the time. What's that all about?

Elizabeth: David is a nice man, and he doesn't get the credit he deserves for everything he does here.

David: Neither do you, Elizabeth. I think that deep down Betty knows you're an excellent business manager and market analyst.

Elizabeth: Well… She doesn't seem to value any of us at all.

Tim: You're right about that, Elizabeth, Betty doesn't really value any of us; and that had better change soon!

But that doesn't explain those matching rings. What's the story there? Huh? *[Leers a bit?]*

Elizabeth: Oh, these? David bought one when he was in Hamilton on holidays last year. I admired it, so I ordered one like it. It's just a coincidence, Tim. We both happen to like the same rings.

Tim: Yeah sure.

Scene 7 *[after dinner but before dessert]*

Betty: Well, everybody, the time has come to light up the New Year's Eve poster! When the room lights go down, everyone who has a popper can go ahead and pull it, and you can blow those noisemakers all you want, too. **But wait until the room lights go down** before pulling and blowing! And maybe in the sharing spirit of the New Year, those of you who have poppers can get a friend or partner who doesn't have one to pull your popper with you...

Elizabeth, Tim, and David, you three usually help with the lighting ceremony. And Geri, why don't you join us, too?

[Elizabeth, Tim, David, and Geri all gather around the poster]

Betty: And now can we have the room lights off, please! *[After lights go down]* Okay, folks, let's pull those poppers and blow to your heart's content!!

Sound cue: play "Happy New Year [by Abba]" or some other song that isn't "Auld Lange Syne" reasonably loudly!

> *There is total confusion in the dark,*
> - *The sound of poppers going off and noise-makers being blown.*
> - ***Betty*** *applies blood to her neck and is lying on the floor (or sitting in a chair, but propped such that the wound is easy to examine).]*
> - ***Elizabeth*** *removes tinsel garland from poster.*
> - ***Tim*** *gently tips the poster over.*
> - ***Elizabeth*** *dumps the tinsel garland in a pile onto the poster.*
> - ***Geri*** *picks up the knife and sets it on the floor.*
> - ***David*** *shoots gun at poster and places gun on the floor.*
> - *Cast members all shouting and mumbling.*
> - ***Tim*** *is holding his scarf, not wearing it.*

David: *[Checks to make sure everyone else is ready then shouts].* Something doesn't seem right here! Can we please have the lights back on?

Geri: *[Waits for lights to come on. Looks at Betty and shouts almost disgustedly]* Oh No! *[Pause]* Oh, for crying out loud, this is just what I ***don't*** need. It looks as if Betty has been … "shot in the dark". I don't have time for this nonsense.

Tim: Shot! David, you have a gun! Why did you shoot Betty?

David: I didn't! When the lights went off, I felt a shove on my back. I put my hand back there, and my gun was gone! Someone took it from my waistband. I didn't shoot it, and I didn't shoot Betty.

Tim: Yeah, you're probably too much of a wimp to actually kill someone anyway.

Elizabeth: But you aren't, are you, Tim! You knew that gun was there in David's waistband, and you easily could have pushed David, taken his gun, and shot Betty while everyone was popping their poppers and blowing their … things….

Geri: Are we sure she was shot? I mean look – the New Year poster is tipped over. The tinsel garland was clearly removed and then just tossed back onto the poster. Maybe she was strangled with that garland. Or look! Tim isn't wearing his scarf any more, the one he had on when he was singing. He has it in his hand! Maybe he strangled her with that! Nice work, Tim!

Tim: Well, David still has his scarf with him, too. Maybe he strangled her instead of shooting her.

Elizabeth: And the knife has been moved. *[looks and sees it].* Oh look! It's on the floor now! Maybe she was stabbed! And look! David's gun is there on the floor, too!

David: I think she was shot, **and not by me!** However, strangling wouldn't have caused that wound on her neck. And if she'd been stabbed, why isn't there any blood on the knife?

Geri: Maybe the garland or Tim's scarf chafed her neck and caused that wound. *[pause]* Or, maybe she was poisoned?

Elizabeth: Poisoned? How and when?

Geri: The frosting on the cake! She dipped her finger into that, remember, and said it tasted worse than usual! Anyone could have poisoned it before David brought it in.

Tim: That would have poisoned any one of us, not just her. *[Gasp]* or maybe **all** of us! I'm not touching that cake now. *[to Audience]* Don't eat the cake, people!

Elizabeth: *[pondering]* David, I think you're right. She was probably shot, but how do we know which one of us shot her? There are so many possibilities. Tim, you seem to be a popular choice. You were angry because she was delaying your promotion. Did you shoot her?

Tim: Hey, I didn't like her, but she paid me well. Also, I respected her business skills and admired her toughness. Yes, I was upset that she wasn't promoting me fast enough, but I was already exploring other career options. I didn't need her. Besides, if I killed her, who's to say I'd be promoted after that? Huh? So, no, I didn't kill her…. But Geri, she threatened you pretty seriously tonight. Maybe you killed her.

Geri: I wasn't bothered by her threats. We were just negotiating, that's all. But what about this nicey-nice lady *[indicating Elizabeth]*? Betty was seriously on her case tonight for not getting the sales forecasts perfect, and she was feeling as if Betty didn't give her proper recognition for all she did in the firm.

Tim: Speaking of proper recognition, David was always defending Elizabeth, and she was always talking about how much **he** was under-appreciated. Maybe Mr. Wimp here grew a pair and did it himself, but pretended someone else took the gun from his waistband.

David: *[Sneezes, but into his elbow, not his handkerchief!]* Everyone here had good reason to be happy that Betty is dead. But instead of speculating wildly, let's see if we can solve this murder. We'll put all the evidence we can find up here on this table. Then each of you come up and look at the body **without touching it!** And look at the evidence. Then fill out your suggestion slips: Who killed Betty the Batchly and how?

Evidence list:
- *Gun from floor*
- *Knife from floor*
- *Poster tipped over*
- *Garland dumped onto poster*
- *Tim's scarf*
- *David's scarf*
- *fruitcake*
- *Also on the table: fax, rum, and cigarette lighter [Hint: make sure the rum is heavily guarded even if it is fake!]*

Denouement
[David makes sure he has only bloody handkerchief ready.]

Elizabeth: Okay, everyone. Let's face it. We all liked having our jobs, and we all liked the paycheques from Arttekko, but none of us liked Betty. Any one of her employees here in this room had a good, strong motive for killing her. Even __AUD #4__ here could have killed her. S/he was bad-mouthing Betty all night. Where were you, **AUD #4**, when the lights went out? *[Check with AUD#4's seat neighbours for verification; maybe even grill **AUD #4** a bit].*

Geri: So are you folks saying we'll have to stay here and give witness statements for the cops? Well, I'm not sticking around for all this silliness. I'm a busy woman, and I have more important things to do. *[begins to slowly collect her belongings but doesn't leave.].*

David: *[sneezes again, and without thinking, pulls bloody handkerchief out to blow his nose].*

Elizabeth: Bless you.

David: Thank you, Elizabeth.

Geri: What is this, you two? Some kind of love fest?

Tim: Hey, everyone! Look at David's handkerchief! It has blood all over it!

Geri: Tim is right! David, how did your handkerchief get all bloody? It was perfectly clean when you blew your nose earlier this evening.

Tim: Well, not clean, Geri. He *did* blow his nose in it a couple of times.

Elizabeth: David is very susceptible to getting bloody noses, right David? *[pause]* David??

David: Thanks for trying, Elizabeth. But no, I'm not susceptible to getting nosebleeds. I think it's time to fess up.

Elizabeth: *[rushing to David]* No, David! Don't!

David: *[Brushing off Elizabeth.]*. It's no use Elizabeth. The rest of you might as well know: Elizabeth and I have had a close relationship now for over seven years. We were married, secretly, three years ago. Betty the Batch would **not** tolerate having employees married to each other, but neither of us wanted to quit our jobs, so we just kept our marriage secret.

Tim: What a couple of idiots! Everybody at Arttekko knew you two had something going. Why didn't you just live together and not get married?

David: *[angry]* Don't call us idiots. We seriously considered that, but we knew that living common law would mean we'd have been married legally after only three years. Betty the Batch wouldn't have tolerated that either.

Elizabeth: David kept a small apartment that he used once in awhile, and we've been car-pooling to work together ever since I joined Arttekko, so no one suspected we were leaving together from my apartment every morning to come to work.

Tim: We all *[gestures to audience]* **knew** there was something going on between you two. You didn't hide it very well. Betty knew, too. She even asked me about it just last week.

Elizabeth: And I'm sure you were happy to fan the flames of suspicion, weren't you, Tim. Anything to get ahead in the firm.

Geri: Whoa! Enough! I need to get out of here, so can we go back to the murder? Tell us about the blood on your handkerchief, David.

David: I was becoming increasingly upset with Betty the Batch. And tonight when she so rudely ordered me around in front of everyone and then criticized Elizabeth in front of everyone, too, I resolved to kill her. When the lights went out, I was ready to reach for my gun, but just then, someone shoved me. They must have taken my gun then.

Geri: That was me. I knew she would report that I was accepting pay-offs and padding my expense account for letoM Motels, and I couldn't let her do that. So I pushed you and took the gun. I hesitated a moment or so, and then I was bumped just as I fired the gun. I thought I'd shot her anyway, but, David if you have blood on your handkerchief, maybe something else happened.

Tim: I think you missed her, Geri. While you were getting the gun from David, I was trying to take the tinsel garland from around the poster so I could strangle her. That Batch...ly wasn't going to promote me and I wanted revenge. But just as I got the garland off the poster, the gun went off and the poster fell down. I panicked and threw the garland back onto the poster. I never had a chance to strangle the Batch...ly.

Elizabeth: So that's when you took your scarf off! You still were going to try to strangle her! And Geri's shot from David's gun must have hit the poster, knocking it over. I knew you didn't shoot her, David!

David: You're right, Elizabeth! There's a bullet lodged into the frame, right here *[indicating bullet in the wooden poster frame].*

Geri: Exactly what did you do after I took your gun, David?

David: I could tell Betty hadn't been hit by the gunshot because she was still babbling about something as the poster fell.

[turns to Elizabeth] Darling, I couldn't take it anymore. She was never very pleasant to me in spite of everything I did for the company. And she didn't treat you any better. Yesterday she confronted me about our relationship. I denied everything, of course, to save our jobs, but she seemed even more menacing than usual. After she publicly criticized your work tonight, I snapped. I'm sorry.

Tim: Hey, the wimp has a pair after all! Way to go, David! What happened? How'd you do it?

David: You're the smart guy with the biz-skool degree. You haven't figured it out yet?

[pause]

Elizabeth: When you realized Geri's shot missed her, that's when you picked up the knife and stabbed her, right? *[David nods]* And then you wiped the knife clean with your handkerchief, right? *[David nods]* and when you tried to put the knife back on the table, it fell onto the floor. *[David nods again]* And the first time you sneezed after stabbing her, you remembered to sneeze into your elbow, not your handkerchief, but this second time you forgot and pulled out the bloody handkerchief.

David: I always knew you were the real brains here at Arttekko, Elizabeth, but now I'll have to leave. Will you go to the police station with me? I think they'll go easy on me when we call this entire roomful of witnesses to testify that Geri and Tim and **AUD#4** were all trying to kill her, too.

Elizabeth: I'll go with you, David, but not to the police station. Over the years, I've been putting away our retirement savings. We can transfer those to a bank in the Caribbean and find an island to live on there where we can retire together. Let's get out of here before the police are called. *Elizabeth takes David's arm and leads him out the door.}*

Tim: *[lewd leer]* Say, Geri you know any places around here to go .. bowling?

Geri: Zip it up, Tim. You'd have to kill me first. *[exits].*

Tim: *[shouting after Geri]:* Hey, I'm not into that sort of thing, Geri, but if *you* are, there's a body here in the room.... *[exits]*

*** The End ***

Solution:

David did it with the knife. He had two motives: (1) he couldn't take her badgering him and Elizabeth; (2) also, he became concerned when Betty confronted him about his relationship with Elizabeth. Before the denouement, the audience will likely be aware of only the first one because the second one is revealed only in the denouement.

Props

General:
- Dozens (? Some? Urge customers to bring/provide their own?) of poppers/crackers and noise makers (make sure to include some horns).
- Crappy mass-produced art to show Arttekko's products

David's responsibility *[he'll need help before the show, obviously]*:
- Small(ish?) battery powered lights around a poster with "~~2019~~ 2020", or [~~this year~~ next year] on it, and with bullet lodged in the frame holding the poster up. Lights don't have to work, actually, since they're never turned on during the show.
- Tinsel garland around the edge of the poster. Make sure this is easy to remove.
- Fax from Redner Hotels
- 6 sets of **small** Jingle bells, scarves, dark glasses, and top hats for song (for David, Tim, and 4 AUD).
- Carrot for song
- Gun
- Frosted fruitcake
- Knife for cutting fruitcake
- Handkerchief with blood smeared on it for David
- Clean handkerchief for David
- Rum
- Cigarette lighter

Tim:
Betty: Thick blood for neck.
Geri: Business cards
Elizabeth:
Elizabeth and David:
- Matching rings

Audience Participation and Role Cards

AUDs #1 and #4 are chosen during the show.
AUDs #2 and #3 are chosen during the pre-show mingling
Also members of The Artichokes are chosen during pre-show mingling

Audience Card #1

Go up to Geri Eliot of letoM Motels and ask, "Excuse me, Geri. How did LetoM get its name?"
Do this <u>now</u> and BE VERY LOUD

Audience Card #2 Role Card

Your role: You are Geraldine Eliot's husband. She is a purchasing agent for letoM Motels, a major hotel chain. She has dragged you here because Arttekko is her best business connection, and it will look good for her if you are with her. You know that Geraldine has been taking bribes from suppliers and padding her expense account. You know it's wrong, but the money is good. At the end, Geri will leave. It happens often that she leaves parties early, expecting you to find your own way home.

During the show also give **AUD #2** this **AUD** PARTICIPATION card:

[**Stand up and be loud**] Well, let's not be hasty, Geri. Betty was just checking to see if I had any loose change in my pockets. And later, that position we were in?... remember we were playing Twister. It wasn't what it looked like.
Do this <u>now</u>

Audience Card #3

Your role: You are Tim Jones's wife. He's a philanderer, but you don't mind. You two have an "open" marriage and like to swing in threesomes or with other couples. At one point in the evening, Tim will cue you. When he does, stand up and shriek very loudly:

> What? You mean Tim **hasn't** been working late every night this past month the way he said? Tim, you scoundrel! You've been out bowling again, haven't you! You dirty donkey! You promised you wouldn't do that anymore ......*[pause, smile flirtatiously]*.... not without taking me along. *[She and Tim laugh together and sit down].*

Be loud, and do NOT show this card to anyone else.

Audience #4 is selected at the time called for in the script. There is no Audience card for AUD #4.

Possible attachment for fronts of the top hats:

Winter Wonderland Lyrics and Dance Steps

Sleigh bells ring, *[left foot out and back]* are you listening *[left foot out and back]*
In the lane, *[right foot out and back]* snow is glistening *[right foot out and back]*
A beautiful sight *[empty hand up above eyes, as if peering]*
We're happy tonight
Walking in a winter wonderland *[walking in place]*

Gone away *[left foot out and back]* is the bluebird *[left foot out and back]*
Here to stay *[right foot out and back]* is a new bird *[right foot out and back]*
He sings a love song *[empty hand over heart]*
As we go along
Walking in a winter wonderland *[walking in place]*

[The Artichokes put on hats, then Tim puts a carrot in David's mouth]

> In the meadow we can build a snowman
> And pretend that he is Parson Brown
> He'll say, Are you married?
> We'll say, No man

David *[Stops The Artichokes (and stops the audience if they are singing along). When they are quiet, David removes the carrot from his mouth and continues (speaking or singing the line here)]* That last line we sang was "He'll say, 'Are you married? We'll say, No man.'"

Okay, Tim, you're on!

Tim: *[sings solo]* "Cuz all we want to do is fool around."

David: Everyone now *[same dance steps]*:

> Later on, we'll perspire
> As we dream by the fire
> To face unafraid *[hands cup each side of face]*
> The plans that we've made
> Walking in a winter wonderland

Other holiday variations:

- **Christmas Party:** a Christmas tree instead of a poster. See the first script in this book.

- **Valentine's Day**: A giant heart with red lights and garlands around the outside edge; possible song "Let me call you sweetheart"; hearts on top hats, heart-shaped eyeglasses, red scarves.

- **St. Patrick's Day**: A giant shamrock with green lights and garland around the outside edge; possible songs: march in to "It's a long way to Tipperary" and then sing "When Irish Eyes are Smiling". Shamrocks on hats or green hats; green lens glasses; green scarves.

- **Victoria Day**: A giant empty 2-4 with white lights around it and a silver garland; possible song "Canada" or "Roll out the Barrel". Canadian flags on top hats or red & white hats, or maybe even pictures of Queen Elizabeth on the hats; red lens glasses; red or red & white scarves.

- **Hallowe'en:** A giant pumpkin with orange streamers, garlands, and lights around it; possible song "The Monster Mash" or "Witch Doctor" or?. Jack-o-lanterns on top hats.

An Introduction to Producing and Performing Mystery Dinner Theatre Shows

I have been involved with the theatre much of my life, and I began performing in mystery dinner theatre shows over twenty years ago. From the outset, I was in love with the genre, mostly because for mystery dinner theatre performances, you must be (hah! You *get* to be) the character the entire time – during the cocktail hour, during the meal, between scenes, and right up through the concluding scene, where the solution is worked out (traditionally called the Denouement).

All of the mystery dinner theatre shows I have been involved with have been comedies. The goal is for everyone, including the actors, the audiences, the wait staff, and the caterers to have a lot of fun.

The scripts are merely the basis for the story. The fun for the actors and the audience comes from both the performances and the interactions. But even though there is always a lot of improv-ing and ad-libbing going on throughout the performance, it is important that the actors learn the scripts carefully. Actors do not have to be proficient at improv theatre to be great at mystery dinner theatre; so long as everyone develops a careful, consistent back-story for their character, then interacting in character flows naturally.

The Timing and Structure
of a Mystery Dinner Theatre Show

The Evening of the Performance. If possible before the audience arrives, solution slips and pencils should be put around at each place on the tables. If the audience has already arrived or is already arriving, do this as quietly and as quickly as possible, trying not to interact with the audience unless it can be done in character somehow, in which case it is a great way to introduce your character to the audience.

Cocktails. The shows usually begin with an informal cocktail time that can last anywhere from fifteen minutes up to over an hour. Make sure that host/sponsors who hire/invite your troupe to perform a script understand that this is an important part of the performance.

During the cocktail hour, the actors enter the room and begin mingling, *always staying in character.* They let people know who they are and why they are there, and they try to learn and remember the names of at least a few of the people in the audience. It is usually the case that knowing the names of just a few audience members and then referring to them by name later makes the shows more enjoyable for everyone.

Different companies have different rules about whether actors can drink during the show. Some say "No drinking at all; it looks unprofessional." Others leave it up to each actor to use their own good judgement. One company actually pays the actors cash in advance on the way to the venue so they can buy drinks if there is a cash bar there. My own preference is that I don't drink before or during a show, but I might happily join in if there is wine provided with the meal.

Scenes. The scenes should be reasonably well-spaced, but the actual timing of the scenes will depend on the type of meal that is being served. Often the first scene or two are performed after people are seated but before any appetizers or salads are served. If the meal is served buffet style, it is generally not a good idea to try to perform any scenes while people are getting their food. During buffets is another great time for the actors to mingle and interact, playing off the material that was introduced in the first two or three scenes.

If at all possible, make sure that desserts are not served or put out before the murder scene is completed.

It is nearly always helpful to have a short break between scenes. This break can be anywhere from just a half minute or so up to five or more minutes, again depending on the audience and the type of meal. Actors should use these breaks to mentally refresh what scene will come next and especially to interact with the audience. The break between scenes is *not* designed so the actors can leave the room to review lines for the next scene.

Evidence. During the murder scene, the evidence is collected and placed on an evidence table. Feel free to let the audience members examine the evidence, but be careful if guns or bottles of alcohol are involved. ***Audience members must not be allowed to handle guns (even if they are unloaded), sharp knives, bottles of alcohol, etc.*** I have been in too many performances where some audience member tries out the gun or tries to steal the bottle of alcohol (even if it is fake).

Guard the Corpse. Following the murder scene, audience members are also invited to examine the corpse *without touching it*. One of the actors must be assigned to guard the corpse very carefully. I can't count the times people have kicked a foot or tried to poke or tickle the corpse. A guard for the body is imperative. One company that I have worked with puts out small pylons around the corpse to try to reduce these problems, but even that strategy doesn't always work.

Collect Solution/Suggestion Slips. With one actor guarding the corpse, one actor guarding the evidence, and one actor as the victim, then two other actors are left to collect the solution slips from the audience. Once the audience members have finished looking at the body and the evidence, the guards can also help collect the solution slips.

It really helps whoever is directing the performance if the solution slips are sorted (not in any obvious manner) while they are being collected into three categories: correct solutions, funny or amusing or audience-related solutions that the rest of the audience might enjoy, and all the rest.

After the Denouement. You may want to present prizes or certificates for the people who get the correct solution. Prizes and certificates aren't necessary, but if you have them, wait until the end of the show to prepare them so that there isn't too long a gap between collecting the slips and moving on to the denouement (concluding scene).

Guide for Actors:

Learn your lines! Mystery Dinner Theatre involves a considerable amount of improv-type work and ad-libbing with the audience, but you cannot improv your way through the script. Your fellow actors are counting on you to learn your lines and feed them proper cues. Also, learn the direction and the cues that others will be providing for you, and familiarize yourself with the lines in all the scenes. The more you know about the rest of the play, and not just your own lines, the smoother the production will be.

Before your first performance, **develop your back-story**. Who are you? Where did you come from? What are your relationships with the other characters? Try to anticipate questions and comments your character will get from the audience so you'll be better prepared and can provide a richer, more enjoyable performance.

Before the cocktail hour (if possible, or else during it), help put out the solution slips and pencils.

Stay in character. Feel free to ad-lib now and then, but generally it is a good idea to let your fellow actors know about any prepared ad-libs you develop. Make sure you don't throw them off by deviating too far from the script, and make sure you get the cue lines right.

Look and act guilty, even if you aren't! Every character in the play must look guilty so that the solution isn't obvious to the members of the audience.

Engage! Know and understand the theme of the show and make sure every audience member understands it, too. Try to get them to play along with the theme.

Between scenes, go from table to table to engage with different members of the audience. Yes, you may eat, but your main role is to be a part of the show, speaking with the audience members.

Guard. Prior to the murder scene, be clear about who will be guarding the body and who will be guarding the evidence, and do not leave your guard duty until you are sure that audience members will no longer be coming up to look at them.

Help. During the murder scene, collect the evidence (as called for in each script) and put it on the evidence table.

Help collect and sort the solution slips.

After the introductions, help the Director identify and thank the audience members who participated. And then after the show be sure to mingle with the audience (as yourself, not in character).

And finally help collect everything for your next show.

Guide for Directors:

Once you have booked a show, **cast it**. If you're not sure about actor availability, cast the show before you confirm booking it.

The age ranges in these scripts are suggestions. Judicious use of costuming, wigs, makeup, and props can go a long way. In the companies I have worked with, I have seen the same actor play a 17-year-old high school quarterback in one script and then the next month play an 80-year-old dodderer in a different script.

Make sure the actors know what is expected of them.

Meet with the host/sponsor, or be sure to discuss the details of the performance with them on the phone or by email. Make clear before booking the show that meals must be provided for all the cast members. Explain how mystery dinner theatre shows work if they don't already know, and go over the meal format. Emphasize the importance of not serving desserts until after the murder scene, no matter what the format for the rest of the meal.

Arrange for all the proper costumes and props (for instance, the office party scripts provided here involve quite a few props that must be prepared in advance).

Hold rehearsals. Typically, the companies I have worked with have held only one rehearsal per script per season. That's right! Just one rehearsal (beats the heck out of community theatre in that regard!). Others have held as many as two or three rehearsals for each performance, but never more than three that I can recall.

During rehearsals invite the actors to describe their characters. Help them work up their back-stories. Discuss their costume plans and options.

Just before each performance have a full script run-through. Sometimes this can be done in the car on the way to the performance venue. If time permits, go over the murder scene and the denouement scene a second time because those are the scenes that usually need the most work.

Learn the order of the scenes. Until I have done a show many times, I actually keep a little cheat sheet outlining the scenes in my pocket to help me remember the scene order. Getting the scenes out of order unfortunately can occur, and it can really confuse the audience and the rest of the actors.

Confirm with the sponsor or host when you are ready to begin the show.

Confirm with each actor with a glance or nod when you are ready to begin each scene. Don't let the gap between scenes get too long.

Help whoever is opening a scene **get the audience's attention**. This is an important task.

During the performances, **monitor** the volume and let actors know if they need to speak louder. Also, if there are flubs, brain freezes, or other problems, **help** get things back on track if necessary.

When the performance is concluded,
- Introduce the cast
- Explain the solution
- Read the amusing suggested solutions (optional)
- Read the names of the people who had the correct solutions.
- Identify and thank all the audience members who participated.
- Optional: Award certificates or prizes (or draw for a prize)
- Thank the audience.
- Mingle with the audience.

Audience Participation

What really makes mystery dinner theatre shows successful is the fun that audience members have, either participating or watching their friends participate. In each of these scripts (and in every one I've ever performed in) there are **Audience Cards** that set out a task for a particular audience member. The task will typically say, "go up to [X character] and ask ...". The audience cards are a great way to increase audience involvement but they also can play an important role of letting the audience as a whole know that a new scene is about to begin.

Other audience participation involves **Role Cards**. These are usually handed to people during the cocktail hour and they instruct them to adopt a certain role and play that role throughout the show. For example, in the Office Party scripts, several audience members are selected as spouses for the characters.

Some companies laminate the audience cards and role cards and try to make sure they get them back after each show. Others print new ones (actually they're called cards, but they're just slips of paper) for each show.

General

No matter how hard we work on our volume, **we can almost always be louder**. During mystery dinner theatre shows, especially those held during holiday seasons, audiences drink. Sometimes they talk loudly, and sometimes they kibitz in the extreme. Everyone should do their best to make sure the actors are heard and that the show moves along. It is not acceptable to tell audience members to 'shut up'. Find some other way of dealing with the situation.

There is a real tendency when you are speaking to another character to approach them or even to go nearer to them; but when that happens, an actor's volume almost inevitably drops. It is difficult, but try to stay on opposite sides of the room (or at least quite apart) from the actors with whom you are interacting. Staying apart from each other induces you to speak louder; it also helps you know if audience members near you don't hear a line, and you can ask (in character, of course) the other actor to repeat it.

Although scripts like these are written to be performed at and during dinner, they can readily be adapted for tea parties or cocktail parties.

Every script I've performed in, like these, contains sexual innuendo in varying degrees. Make sure your host/sponsor understands this, and depending on the nature of your audience be prepared to tone it down. It's tempting sometimes to go overboard with the ad-libbing in this area, but control the urge.

Related to that, **do not swear**. It detracts from the humour, and some audience members will find it offensive. Maybe a hell or a damn might creep in, but try not to use even those words.

Do not touch audience members unnecessarily or inappropriately. Even what you think of as an innocent placing of a hand on someone's shoulder or arm should be avoided. If you're mutually attracted with a member of the audience, don't go home with them that night. Don't even suggest it!

Keep things moving. As my early mentor Brian March once wrote, "If the guests aren't talking, make sure you are," especially around the dinner table.

Solution Slips

Audience members should have pre-printed solution slips at their places. It's nice if you can provide pencils, too, but generally enough guests will have pens or pencils that they can get by on their own. The solution slips should roughly look like this:

Your Name: _____

Who Committed the Murder: _____

Weapon: _____

Motive: _____

[Note: not all mystery dinner theatre companies ask people to specify the motive. Asking for a motive tends to reduce the number of people who get the correct solution.]

Acknowledgements:

I am forever grateful to the companies I have worked for over the years, performing in mystery dinner theatre shows:

    Brian March and Mystery Unlimited
    A group in Clinton, Ontario, Murder Incorporated
    Kay Rogers and Murder for Hire
    John Darnell and Gumshoe Mysteries

Working with all the actors in these groups and learning different things from each of them has been wonderful.

I also want to thank my wife, Carolle Trembley, who has helped me learn lines for so many plays over the past twenty-plus years.

If the idea of hosting a mystery dinner theatre show appeals to you, by all means get in touch with Gumshoe Mysteries, the company with which I am currently involved. Their website indicates most of the scripts they will be happy to perform.

And if you aren't somewhat near southwestern Ontario but would like to see more scripts, both John Darnell and Kay Rogers will be able to help you.

There are thousands of mystery scripts out there waiting to be performed. Why should you use these scripts or scripts from Gumshoe Mysteries?
- Because the format is tried, tested, and proven. The shows are a roaring success with many sponsors booking different scripts the following year and many audience members booking shows for their own groups.
- Because the scripts are so readily adaptable. I have been in shows with over 400 hundred people in the audience (yes, we were miked and had sound engineers) or as few as eight in a small house party. While the shows are ordinarily performed in restaurants, we've done them on cruise ships, on trains, in church basements, at golf courses, you name it.

If you have any questions, I am on Facebook as John Palmer, my email address is EclectEcon@gmail.com or my blog is at www.eclectecon.net

Break legs!